LIKE A TIGER WITH HIS PREY,
HE HAD TOLERANTLY ALLOWED HER
TO MAINTAIN HER DISTANCE . . .

Now hard arms wrapped themselves around her, and his head bent to hers. In that instant before their mouths met, the rain drummed on the roof and her heart accelerated to match its primitive cadence. Her hands went of their own accord to his back and telegraphed their disturbing message of cool, sleek skin. She arched her back to press against him, seeking the pleasure she remembered from a million dreams. Then his lips closed over hers, warm and male and demanding. . . .

A CANDLELIGHT ECSTASY ROMANCE ®

SURRENDER TO THE NIGHT

Shirley Hart

A CANDLELIGHT ECSTASY ROMANCE®

Published by
Dell Publishing Co., Inc.
1 Dag Hammarskjold Plaza
New York, New York 10017

Dell ® 681510, Dell Publishing Co., Inc.

Candlelight Ecstasy Romance ®, 1,203,540, is a registered
trademark of Dell Publishing Co., Inc.,
New York, New York.

ISBN: 0-440-18473-8

Printed in the United States of America
First printing—May 1983

To Our Readers:

We have been delighted with your enthusiastic response to Candlelight Ecstasy Romances®, and we thank you for the interest you have shown in this exciting series.

In the upcoming months we will continue to present the distinctive sensuous love stories you have come to expect only from Ecstasy. We look forward to bringing you many more books from your favorite authors and also the very finest work from new authors of contemporary romantic fiction.

As always we are striving to present the unique absorbing love stories that you enjoy most—books that are more than ordinary romance.

Your suggestions and comments are always welcome. Please write to us at the address below.

Sincerely,

The Editors
Candlelight Romances
1 Dag Hammarskjold Plaza
New York, New York 10017

A cool, delicious breeze blew in the open window above the sink, faintly scented with the smell of new-planted corn. From the window Trisha Flannery could see the south field, where the green plants marched across the black Iowa soil in orderly rows. The healthy look of the crop filled her with a sense of pride. She had planted that corn herself, with only Jamie for company, riding along on the tractor. Somehow they had made it through the first planting season, she and her mother and Jamie, without her stepfather.

The setting sun cast a faint golden glow over the tender green plants. She relaxed slightly, feeling the tightness in her muscles drain away. Doing the dishes here in the kitchen with her mother and her sister was a familiar ritual; her hands performed all the motions by themselves. Which was all the more reason she was not prepared for the bombshell her sister decided to drop.

"Jud and I want to adopt Jamie," Margie said.

Carefully Trisha set the bowl she was wiping down on the cupboard and turned to look at her married sister. "Have you thought about all the problems involved?"

Margie, six years older than Trisha's twenty-seven but five

9

inches shorter, straightened to her full petite height, a fiery look in her dark eyes. "Yes, we have. And we still want him."

Her mother, hands immersed in sudsy dishwater in the sink, was strangely silent.

"It's not up to me," Trisha said stiffly. "You know that."

"But you are involved," Margie said earnestly. "We'd be taking Jamie to live with us on the other place if everything goes through okay."

"He's happy here," Trisha countered.

"But he starts to school in the fall. He needs the security of one set of parents. Otherwise there'll be questions about his mother—and his father . . ." Her voice trailed away, but Trisha said crisply, "Jamie has nothing to be ashamed of. He can tell the truth, that they're divorced and his mother lives in Los Angeles and his father is in New York. There's nothing so unusual about that these days."

"Jamie deserves better," Margie said quietly.

Trisha shot back, "Mother and I take good care of him—"

"That's not what I meant, and you know it." There was an obstinacy about Margie that reminded Trisha of a small terrier dog. "Of course he gets good care here, the best," Margie conceded. "That's not the issue. The issue is giving Jamie a home with both a father and a mother."

Virginia Adams sighed. "Girls, stop it. Jamie will hear you."

Margie whirled around to her mother, her cheeks vivid. "We're so close, you could see Jamie anytime you wanted to. It isn't as if we're taking him away from you."

"I know that, dear," Mrs. Adams said gently. "But aren't you forgetting something? It's true your sister Diane doesn't give two pins for Jamie and would readily consent to your adopting him." Her mouth tightened momentarily, and Trisha knew her mother was thinking of her daughter's lack of a sense of responsibility for her own son. Then she seemed to compose herself and said, "But we don't know what Jord's feelings are in the matter."

10

Trisha made a sound in her throat. "Fat lot he cares about Jamie. He hasn't seen him since he was little."

"Don't judge Jord by his actions," her mother said sharply.

Trisha emitted a short, crisp laugh. "*Don't judge Jord by his actions,*" she mimicked. "What am I supposed to judge him by? His good intentions?"

Trisha backed into the familiar triangular corner where the two counters met at right angles and leaned against each side for support, an old and childish habit that had always comforted her. She pushed one hand through her long, black hair and then resumed the attack. "Or should I assume he has an undying affection for his son because of the Christmas and birthday gifts he sends Jamie every year?"

Her mother's face darkened. "That's considerably more attention than your sister pays to her child."

"That's it!" Margie's small face lightened, and a hand went up to push back a curly black tendril. "We'll invite Jord to Jamie's birthday party."

"He won't come." Trisha's voice was flat.

Her mother shot her a speaking look. "You don't know that for sure."

Trisha braced her hands against the smooth counter and said, "I know you've always had a soft spot in your heart for him, Mother, but don't defend him to me."

"Funny," her mother murmured. "I seem to remember you having quite a 'soft spot' in your heart for him one summer, when he stayed here."

Trisha's cheeks flamed. "I was seventeen then. I'm no longer subject to schoolgirl crushes, thank God."

"Aren't you?" her mother murmured.

Trisha's eyes changed to the deep violet that flashed danger like the semaphores on a highway. "What do you want from me? I can't change the fact that Jord Deverone is a ruthless, egotistical bas—"

"Trisha!" Her mother slapped the dishcloth against the edge

11

of the sink. "Jord deserves better than that from you! He's never harmed you in any way." She glared at her daughter for a moment, only to be met with glittering violet eyes that refused to back down an inch. Mrs. Adams opened her mouth as if to say something and then thought better of it and turned back to the sink. Giving it her entire attention, keeping her eyes carefully away from her daughter's hot face, she rinsed away the soap bubbles. Then she said in a more controlled tone, "You'd do well to guard your tongue—especially if Jord does come to Iowa and Margie tries to persuade him to give his permission to adopt."

"And you approve of that?" Trisha's voice skittered upward.

Mrs. Adams turned to face her daughter, her eyes guarded. "Judson loves Jamie, and he's good with him." She seemed to hesitate and then said softly, "I think he'd make an excellent father for Jamie."

Trisha frowned, but Margie was triumphant. "There, you see? Mother agrees with me."

An intolerable tension made Trisha shrug her shoulders. "That's her privilege."

Margie laid a small hand on her arm. "Trish, please. Don't be angry with me about this. You must know how I feel, not being able to have a child. And after all, we're doubly related to Jamie since Judson is Jord's cousin. Jamie even looks like Jud."

The tension flung itself downward to the pit of her stomach. "Look, you do whatever you think is right. I—won't stand in your way." She thrust herself away from the counter. "I wish you luck. Getting in touch with Jord Deverone, entrepreneur and jet-setter, might not be the easiest thing in the world."

"Oh, I have his phone number and address," Margie said airily. "Remember, he gave both his office number and his home number to Mom and me—in case anything happened to Jamie and we needed to contact him."

"Thoughtful of him," Trisha muttered sardonically, stretching her tall, slim body around to hang her towel on the rack.

"Now all you have to do is get past his corps of secretaries and assistants."

Halfway across the country, in a high-rise skyscraper towering over Manhattan, Jord Deverone's assistant, Bradley Hunt, strolled into the anteroom of Jord's office and grinned at the woman sitting behind the desk. "Am I late?"

Dara Kincaid, Jord's secretary, met his eyes. "Let's just say he's been asking for you."

The impish smile faded, replaced by a yawn. "He had me up till three o'clock last night, working on that merger with the microprocessor company in California. I thought I deserved a little shut-eye." He hooked a leg over the corner of Dara's desk familiarly. "What time did he get in this morning—or shouldn't I ask?" He nodded toward the rich walnut double doors.

Dara shrugged, a noncommittal movement of the shoulders. "He was here when I got here."

"The man's got the constitution of a horse. Must be all those summers he spent on the farm as a boy." Brad picked up the glass paperweight from her desk and rolled it in his palm thoughtfully. "What he needs is a woman. What happened to that cute little actress he's been seeing?"

"I haven't the vaguest idea."

The paperweight teetered close to the end of his fingers. "I saw her picture in the paper with some junior congressman." He slid off the desk and replaced the paperweight. "Too bad. She lasted longer than most. I keep thinking if he had a woman, he'd spend the night with her instead of me." He gave her a wide-eyed look. "I mean, it would be better for him if he didn't work every living minute of the day and night, wouldn't it?"

"Self-sacrificing to the end, aren't you?" Dara murmured.

"Dara." Even through the intercom Jord Deverone's voice was crisp with command.

Brad shook his head and put his finger to his lips. Dara calmly ignored him. "Yes, Mr. Deverone?"

13

"Has Brad come in yet?"

Brad rolled his eyes and shook his head violently. "Tell him you haven't seen me since last January," he said in a theatrical whisper.

"Yes, he has," she replied calmly. "Shall I send him in?"

"Please." There was a little click, and the light on the intercom board flashed off.

"Cheer up," Dara said, mock-consoling. "Maybe he's calling you in to tell you you have the weekend off."

"Yeah, sure," Brad answered. "And maybe you'll get awarded the Pulitzer Prize for fiction this year." Dara's soft laugh echoed after him as he walked toward the door.

Brad seldom stepped into Deverone's office suite without wondering what it would be like to sit behind that mahogany desk and wield the power Deverone had at his fingertips. Jord had his finger in seventeen different pies, among them, coal mining in Wyoming, a ranch in Colorado, a private airport in Upstate New York, a newspaper chain in Ohio, an exclusive string of hotels currently going up in Florida. Twenty thousand people depended on the Deverone conglomerate for employment, and Brad was one of them.

Jord didn't waste time questioning him about his lateness—as Brad had known he wouldn't. There was only a brief greeting, and those brown eyes the color and texture of stones flickered over him, and then he nodded toward the chair beside his desk. Brad lowered himself into it, his smile still in place.

"We'll be lunching with Mr. and Mrs. Quinton at Cherrow's at one o'clock." Mentally Brad shrugged off any feeling of being manipulated. He knew from past experience that the lunch could develop into something mildly interesting. Deverone had flown the head of the newspaper chain and his wife in from Cleveland, and Mrs. Quinton was an attractive and vivacious woman in her early thirties. If Jord affected her the way he did most of the woman that came into his orbit, Wilson Quinton might have difficulty concentrating on talk about his newspaper.

Covertly Brad assessed the man sitting in front of him. Was it his physical appearance that made him so attractive to women? Or was it the aura of power and money that women always seemed to be able to detect when it clung to a man? Or was it Jord's own sardonic disregard for the female sex that made them each want to be the one to vault the barrier of those stony eyes and soften their glint of hardness?

Seated at the desk, Jord's six-foot-four frame seemed to dominate the room. Brad had no illusions about the contrast between them. In a smoke-gray suit with a cream shirt, his hair a sun-streaked wheat color, Jord Deverone was the man in charge. He was virile, intelligent, and exuded a subtle, sexual magnetism that made his impact on the opposite sex all the more devastating. He was a man to make any woman's heart beat faster—until she looked into his eyes.

"He's got the figures on the cost of upgrading the printing operation with computers," Deverone went on. "After lunch I want you to go over them carefully and get back to me on it before five o'clock."

"You think you can compete with the *Cleveland Star?*"

Jord glanced up, his eyes narrowed. "I think we'd be fools not to try."

"Quinton's strength is in the homey touch, the in-depth kind of local news."

Jord Deverone's lips twisted. "What's wrong with bringing the homey touch to the people with speed and efficiency?"

"Nothing—if it works."

Jord Deverone relaxed back in his chair. "Technology should increase our communication with one another—not hinder it."

"Yeah, I know." Brad shrugged.

"You don't agree."

Brad shot him a surprised look. Jord had never solicited his opinions before. "Maybe I just want to cling to my own illusions —the harried but dedicated bald-headed editor banging out his

15

story on a Royal portable in the back room just in time to beat the deadline."

Jord's lips curved upward. "That is a fantasy." He seemed to be considering it. "Couldn't you shift your vision just a little and see that bald-headed newspaper man banging out his story on a word processor? Notice he is no longer harried. He now has time to do his editing and still meet his deadline."

"Because his copy is so much easier to change."

Jord nodded. "Of course."

"Just the free flight of his mind rattling over the computer keyboard—"

The intercom buzzed, and Jord, a slight, dry smile on his lips, shifted his gaze away from Brad. Brad watched him, marveling. For a moment he could have sworn that he had brought a flicker of amusement to the other man's eyes.

Dara's voice sounded crisp and efficient through the speaker. "A long distance call for you, Mr. Deverone. A woman named Margie Adams. She says she's your cousin's wife." Even Dara's professional voice couldn't hide the slight note of disbelief in those last few words.

An expression of something—displeasure or irritation, Brad wasn't sure which—flickered across Jord's face. Brad was certain that the call would be refused.

"Put her through." His voice was flat, his face expressionless as he picked up the phone.

Brad would not normally have thought of leaving the room during a telephone call of a personal nature to his boss, but he did now. As if he had read his mind, Jord glanced up. A frown furrowed his brows, and a slight shake of his head told Brad to stay where he was.

"Hello, Margie." The unfamiliar warmth that softened Deverone's voice was in complete contrast to his look of annoyance a moment ago. "Is anything wrong?" There was a genuine concern in the question, as if the unusual nature of the call indicated there

16

might be something very wrong with the woman on the other end of the wire.

Whatever she said evidently relieved his fears, because he relaxed visibly and replied, "I'm glad. And how is Judson?"

Another extended silence. Jord listened, and Brad thought that if there was one thing his boss had, it was the ability to concentrate solely on whatever needed his attention for the moment. Deverone sat still in the chair, his free hand relaxed in front of him. He did not toy with a letter opener or fidget with the pages of the report spread out on his desk. Like a parabolic antenna, his whole body focused on receiving the words from the instrument he held to his ear.

"I really don't think I could work a trip into my schedule, honey."

Honey! His curiosity piqued, Brad watched the other man's face. It had taken on that closed look, the one he knew well. The Deverone poker face—a tight, closed mask that showed nothing of the man's inner emotions, a face Deverone wore during many of his business dealings. Who was this woman? And what was she asking him to do? Whatever it was, it was causing Deverone conflict. He could hear the reluctance to hurt in Jord's voice, see the tightness around his mouth.

Then, surprisingly, a rakish grin lifted Deverone's lips. "Is he really that old already?" Then more seriously, "You know I'd like nothing better than to see him, but I don't see how it's possible."

Brad listened with amazement. Whatever the woman's request was, she hadn't lost the battle yet. Jord was still on the phone, still discussing it with her. With anyone else the conversation would have been terminated seconds ago.

Deverone lowered his voice to a husky, intimate drawl. "I'm afraid the birthday-party scene isn't my thing. What is Jamie interested in these days? I'll send something."

Cousin Margie evidently was vehemently opposed to the idea

of a long-distance gift. Deverone sat listening for several seconds and then said, "You know I wouldn't be welcomed."

Brad held his breath, and a feeling of admiration for the unknown Margie was growing. She'd actually had the courage to call and invite Jord Deverone to some place or event where they both knew he would not be welcomed. Brad marveled at the entire conversation. He'd never heard of this Jamie—but that wasn't surprising. He'd never heard of Cousin Margie, either. If they were family, it was news to him. Not that Deverone's family life was secret—it was simply nonexistent. The man didn't have one. He did have parents—the kind that were easy to live without—divorced, mother living in Mexico, father spending his winters in Arizona, summers on the upper penisula of Michigan. Brad had met them both, liked neither of them. They were cold and calculating; people who seemed interested in their son only because he was a success. Brad had been glad to leave the bright, brittle conversation of Deverone's mother, the frankly probing questions of his father to Jord about the financial state of the conglomerate and escape into fresh air.

"Yes, I know it's the seventeenth of July, and he'll be five." Jord was smiling again, those hard, lean lips lifted in lines foreign to them. "Iowa in July hardly qualifies as a vacation paradise. Did you think I'd forgot how hot it usually is?"

Iowa? Brad shifted in his chair, unable to believe his ears.

There was another long silence, and he guessed that the venerable Margie was pressing her final arguments home. He still had not a clue about Jord's reaction.

Then, with a sudden lithe movement, Jord reached inside his jacket pocket and pulled out the small burgundy leather notebook he used to keep track of his grueling schedule. Brad was thunderstruck. Whatever Margie had, he'd like to bottle and sell it on the streets. They'd both be millionaires. He had never known Jord to be deterred from business by anything personal before.

18

"It's possible I could clear away some of my obligations and spend a few days with you. Let me get back to you."

Jord listened for a few minutes more and then said softly, "I'll call you tonight. Have you changed your number? No? Yes, I have it. All right, I'll call about eleven—it'll be ten there. You'll be home then? Good."

Brad was almost certain Jord had put her off politely—something he never did—until Jord lowered the phone to its cradle and turned those hard, glistening eyes to Brad. "If I do decide to go, I'll want you to go with me."

Brad swallowed. "To Iowa?"

"Yes." The smile played around the hard mouth once again. "What's the matter?" Deverone's eyes missed nothing. He'd seen the convulsive movement of Brad's throat. "Afraid you're letting yourself in for a few days with some hayseed rustics?"

"It isn't that, it's just—well, you're not serious, are you?"

Deverone leaned back in his chair and let his hands relax on the soft leather arms. "We could fly the Learjet to Des Moines and rent a car. It's a three-hour drive from there to Arien."

"Three hours! Isn't there a major airport any closer than that?"

"To that particular corner of northwest Iowa, no." His denial was clipped. "Minneapolis is even farther away. Any objections?"

Brad didn't hesitate. "We're going to fly and drive for six hours just for the privilege of attending a birthday party in the middle of nowhere?"

Jord didn't hide his amusement. "That's right. You aren't afraid of getting lost, are you?"

"I'm more afraid of dying of boredom," Brad drawled.

Jord countered calmly, "You might be in for a shock."

He lifted an eyebrow and grimaced wryly. "A shock of what—oats?"

"So you do know a little about farming." Jord's voice was amused.

"Yeah, I know a little—and that's plenty. I don't want to know any more." He met Deverone's gaze easily. What the hell? He'd already said more than he should. It was only a job. "Tell me something. Is your cousin's wife very attractive?"

Deverone shot him a hard look, his brown eyes gleaming with a sudden animosity. "What made you ask?"

Brad shrugged. Deverone's reaction had been even stronger than he'd imagined it would be. Somehow he'd stumbled into a hornet's nest. But he wasn't going to back down. Doggedly he directed the conversation to the real issue—time. "A minute ago you accused me of clinging to a fantasy. Now you're the one who is fantasizing. You can't possibly fly off to middle America on the seventeenth of July, and you know it. You're due in Switzerland on the thirtieth for that financial meeting, and you'll need a week to prepare, plus a few extra days to fly over ahead of time and get rid of jet lag, and another day or two to sharpen your presentation."

"There'll be time."

Jord leaned back in his chair, apparently relaxed, his face cool and closed, his words sharp with a keen, authorative slice. Brad knew when to stop pressing. He pushed himself up out of the chair. "You said one o'clock for lunch?"

Deverone's gaze was watchful. "Yes." Softly he added, "Too close to breakfast for you?"

It was a subtle reference to his late arrival in the office. Brad ignored it and grinned, good humor restored. "I'll manage." He enjoyed his food, and Deverone knew it. Brad's waist was thickening; he'd tried running but somehow lost interest in it. Though God knew, he shouldn't gain weight working for Deverone. Deverone consistently worked eighteen hours a day, and his lean frame had not a spare ounce of fat on it.

"You can ride with me." Jord was back to normal, cool, authorative. "We'll leave at twelve thirty." Deverone tilted his head and began to study the papers in front of him, his brow already furrowed in concentration. Knowing he was dismissed,

Brad walked across the thick carpeting, sure that Deverone wouldn't even hear the click of the door closing.

He nodded absently to Dara and walked along the hall to his office. He couldn't believe that Jord Deverone was seriously considering flying to the Midwest for the sole purpose of attending some child's birthday party. The whole thing did not make any sense. He shook his head and pushed open the door to his office. On the eve of a meeting that could make or break him as an entrepreneur, Deverone would be fifteen hundred miles away from his office, taking part in a prosaic celebration of games, ice cream, and cake. Brad sat down at his desk and tried to shrug away his feeling of foreboding. If Jord Deverone wanted to spend a few of his precious days rusticating, he couldn't stop him. He could only wonder . . .

He was still wondering about it when they were shown to an elegant table in a coveted corner window of Cherrow's. He couldn't imagine anything further from a small town in Iowa surrounded by cornfields than this sophisticated and luxurious restaurant, which catered to the rich and successful. The high, domed ceiling was painted gold, and a crystal chandelier hung in glittering splendor from its peak. A windswept, slightly soggy view of the New York skyline was spread before them in an unbroken pane of glass from floor to ceiling.

With an ease born of long practice Jord seated Mrs. Quinton next to the window and sat down beside her, leaving Brad to offer Quinton the place across from his wife on the other side of the table.

"Would you care for a cocktail?" Jord's voice was low, intimate, his smile charming. Mrs. Quinton was dressed in a black suit that looked entirely able to compete with the designer dresses on the women around her. It was cut to show off her voluptuous curves and provided the perfect background for the brilliant red hair she wore twisted in a glossy roll at the back of her head. Her hands were professionally manicured, her voice low and modulated. Her husband could give her twenty years, Brad thought, and he must have chosen his own tie. The sleek woman seated beside Jord would never have selected that monstrosity of slashing diagonal lines to wear with a checked suit.

"Yes, thank you. I'd like some white wine." Carol Quinton flashed a high-voltage smile at Jord.

Brad settled back to watch while Quinton opted for a whiskey sour and continued to study his menu, unperturbed. Brad ordered a gin and tonic and decided he'd better nurse it. He wanted all his wits about him. Jord had his usual Manhattan, which never affected his thinking processes at all.

The waiter came to take their orders, and after he had done so, Quinton folded his arms and looked out at the view from the window for a moment or two. Then his gaze swung to Jord's lean face. "Pretty clever stuff." He nodded his head around him. "Come here often?"

Jord gave him a direct look. "Only when I want to impress the Midwesterners from out of town."

"That can't be a regular occurrence," Wilson Quinton said with a hearty bluffness.

"It happens more often than you might think," Jord countered lightly.

"You have enterprises scattered all over the country, haven't you, Mr. Deverone?" Carol lowered her menu and gazed at him.

"Jord, please." Deverone's lips lifted in a slight smile.

"Then you must call me Carol."

"Have you decided what you'd like to have?" Jord's voice was courteous. Brad wondered if he was the only one who noticed how Jord skirted the issue of his wealth.

A wicked gleam flashed in Carol's eyes. "Yes. I'd like—the *salade aux oranges.*" She looked into Jord's eyes. "The menu says it's a house speciality." She dropped long lashes over her eyes and appeared to be engrossed in studying the menu again.

22

But her words were a bold invitation. "I always like to sample the—local specialities of any area I visit."

"Do you travel frequently?" Jord asked blandly, but Brad knew Jord was aware of the sexual innuendo in the woman's words.

"Not as frequently as I'd like." Every word she uttered was a pleasure to the ear. "Now with—your—involvement in my husband's newspapers perhaps I'll be coming to New York more often."

"I'll look forward to that," Jord said, his words casually polite, his attention leaving her as he turned his head to watch the waiter place the drinks they had ordered on the table.

Admiring Jord's tactful handling of the woman, Brad made his own choice from the menu and reached for the tall glass that contained his drink.

Jord directed a question to Quinton, and the ritual began, the fence and parry, dodge and move of the business luncheon. In direct contrast to his bizarre suit and tie Quinton spoke with articulate skill. He possessed a logical mind, and he presented his arguments well and pressed them home with a finesse Brad found himself admiring. Jord listened with the same intentness of concentration he had displayed two hours ago and, when Quinton asked if he had any questions, probed sharply about the problems of expansion in the tight economy and the rising cost of quick dissemination of the papers. Carol Quinton's bright red mouth was pursed, her green eyes fastened on Jord as she listened avidly to the give-and-take discussion of the upgrading of every aspect of the newspaper chain, from the gathering of news to the bookkeeping and accounting system and the acquisition of new subscribers by a systematic telephone dialing campaign.

At the end of an hour some decisions were made. Jord gave his tentative approval to the cost of computers, providing nothing disastrous turned up in the afternoon of study Brad was to put in, and suggested the telephone campaign proceed with temporary help—to be coordinated with spot commercials on television and radio. He wanted a general policy statement put out to reporters about contact with the public during times of trauma; there were to be no incidents of overzealous reporters pouncing on accident victims or bereaved relatives.

Quinton's amicable face twisted into a scowl. "You can't be serious. I can't hamstring my reporters that way—"

"By asking them to display some common decency in dealing with distraught people?" Jord sliced.

Quinton made a grimace, as if he had something in his mouth that tasted unpleasant. "You know nothing about the newspaper business. It's a dog-eat-dog world out there, and the guy who gets the story first—"

Jord's voice was cool, incisive. "One of the reasons the *News* circulation is down in Cleveland is its poor public image," he said bluntly. "You've got to start upgrading that image—now. More and more people are being turned off by the tactics of the press. I want the *News* to be known as the paper that cares."

Stopped cold by Jord's knowledge of the problem he had attempted to hide from his potential investor, Quinton stared at him in amazement. Then his shrewd sense of the rightness of Jord's words surfaced. "The paper that cares—" His voice trailed away as he stared at Jord. "My God. I think you've got something."

"I'll need that policy statement by tomorrow morning," Jord reminded him implacably.

The skirmish was over. Jord had won. Quinton gave his grudging agreement and promised to develop a policy statement and have it in Jord's office by tomorrow morning. When they rose to leave, Jord's face wore the satisfied look that Brad had come to recognize. The meeting had been successful on all counts. Jord had gotten what he wanted. They parted amicably with the Quintons, agreeing to see them in the morning. Only Brad saw the annoyed look on Carol Quinton's face as Jord walked away. When the luncheon was over and his business concluded, Carol

24

Quinton had ceased to exist for Jord Deverone. He had won that skirmish, too.

But that night as Brad sat on Jord's luxurious white leather couch in his condo overlooking the East River, a drink in one hand, the reports of last year's deficits of the *News* in the other, the buzzer on Jord's intercom sounded.

After flashing a cool, puzzled look at Brad, Jord pressed a lean finger on the intercom beside his telephone. The doorman's voice came over the speaker. "Lady here to see you, Mr. Deverone. Says she's a friend of yours. Name's Carol Quinton."

Jord's hesitation was long enough so that even the woman waiting below had to be aware of time sliding by. "Let her come up," he said at last. Without missing a beat he asked Brad, "What was the number of new subscribers for July? Twenty?"

Carefully Brad said, "Yes, that's right." His mind was not on the number of people subscribing to the *News*. This was decidedly a new wrinkle. None of the women who had been attracted to Jord had ever bearded the lion in his den on the strength of a brief encounter at lunch and with so little encouragement.

The soft chime of the doorbell echoed through the apartment. Jord didn't look up from the report. The chime sounded again. Jord gave Brad a brief glance, his face totally bland, and then tossed the report down on the table. His lithe body moving easily in the comfortable jeans and soft shirt he wore, he rose and strode across the beige carpeting of the spacious living room to climb the four steps that led up to the entryway.

The low feminine voice seemed to burst into words the moment Jord opened the door. None of it was intelligible, nor was Jord's low answer, although Brad could hear the cool politeness in his boss's tone.

Carol had evidently handed Jord her raincoat and now stood poised at the top of the steps. Her glance roamed avidly around the room . . . and came to an abrupt stop on him.

Brad smiled. "Hello, Mrs. Quinton. This is a pleasant surprise."

"Yes, isn't it?" she said conventionally, but her eyes were brilliant with anger at finding him there. After an instant's hesitation she extended a shapely leg and descended the stairs, her head high. The silky green dress she wore brushed her knees seductively, outlined her full, feminine curves.

Jord had recently purchased a set of modular furniture, and it was in the middle of that that they had spread their papers. Moving easily behind her down the stairs, Jord invited her to sit down, and Carol Quinton settled on the armless cushion at the end, as if she were a frequent visitor, and opened the small black handbag she carried. After a moment's search she brought out a cigarette. Jord stood watching, a quirk of amusement playing over his mouth as she leaned forward to pick up the table lighter and flick it to life.

"Would you like a drink, Carol, something warming after being out in the rain—a brandy, perhaps?" Jord asked.

"That would be lovely, thank you." A stream of blue smoke accented her words. "I must apologize for dropping in on you like this," she said to his back as he walked to the drinks cabinet in the corner of the room. "Wilson bumped into an old confrere of his from *New York News* days, and they decided to go out and have a drink together." A long, eloquent silence followed her little speech, the only sound in the room the slight clink of glass against glass as Jord poured her drink.

Jord crossed the room and handed her the delicate globe with the amber liquid. She took it, her eyes openly inviting him to sit on the cushion beside her. Coolly he turned and strolled to the armless seat farthest away from her.

Carol was not deterred by his rejection. "Since I was alone in the city, I took the liberty of calling on the only other person I know. I—didn't imagine you might still be working. I am interrupting, aren't I?"

"Yes," Jord said softly, leaning back and watching her. "You are. Your husband wants a decision by nine o'clock tomorrow, and that requires our rather careful study of several reports—

which will take us most of the night." His soft tone took some of the sting from the words, but the iron was there, under the velvet.

Carol Quinton laughed, a low husky sound of feminine amusement, and took a sip of the brandy. Setting the glass on the table beside the chair, she said, "I'm sure Wilson will take your answer whenever you're ready to give it to him. After all, he's coming to you for money, not the other way around." Her eyes moved over Jord's relaxed lean body, their green depths glittering with a sensual hunger Brad had never seen in a woman's eyes. Jord saw it, too, and his face hardened into stone.

As if she were suddenly aware that she had revealed too much, she veiled her eyes with gold-tipped lashes and turned to lay her cigarette in the onyx ashtray beside her. She wore her hair loose tonight, and it lay in a shimmering array over her shoulders. It was hair that invited a man's hand to touch it. The woman was undeniably attractive. Brad was not so sure he could have turned her aside had she decided to pursue him.

"Surely you can afford to take a few hours off," she persisted in that smoky voice. "Perhaps you'll allow me to return your hospitality at lunch today and let me take you out and buy you a drink. I'm sure Mr. Hunt could carry on in your absence."

"I'm sorry. That's not possible." Jord was direct, succinct.

"Not possible—or not what you want to do?" She gave him a direct look, and Brad gave her full marks for poise under fire.

"Both—Mrs. Quinton." The accent on her title was unmistakable.

A flicker of admiration came into her eyes, and she leaned back against the cushion holding the brandy carelessly, a smile playing over her lips. "I didn't know men with old-fashioned ideas of fidelity like yours still existed, Mr. Deverone." She sipped her brandy and rested the foot of the glass goblet on the palm of her hand.

"There are a few of us around."

Carol Quinton was quiet for a moment, her gaze fastened on

the shimmering liquid in her glass. "Somehow at lunch today I got a—different impression."

"Did you?" he asked coolly.

"An impression you purposely created," she shot back just as coolly.

"I think you misread a few acts of courtesy," he countered blandly.

She sat still for a moment and then dropped her eyes, her whole body submissive. It was a complete change of attitude. "Right now I feel very—alone. I need to be with someone."

She was playing on his sympathy as a woman alone in a strange city, and her soft feminine appeal was the most potent weapon in her arsenal.

Jord was not moved. "I did say I was sorry," he reminded her softly.

Her tactics blocked in every direction, she raised her eyes and sent him a look of pure hatred. "If my husband didn't need your money, I'd tell you just exactly what kind of an arrogant bastard you are."

His eyes took on the familiar look of glossy brown stones. "I find your concern for your husband—touching—but slightly belated." His eyes narrowed. "Or did you come here tonight to insure my affirmative answer to him tomorrow morning?"

"You think you own the world, don't you?" She flung the words at him, her pale complexion flaming with temper.

"No," he denied softly, "I only own my little corner of it—no more. But I do have the right to decide how I'll spend my time—and with whom I'll spend it." He met her gaze steadily. In a soft, lethal tone he added, "And I don't want to spend any of it with you, Mrs. Quinton."

The silence that followed the blunt statement seemed to ring through the apartment and reverberate in Brad's ears. Carol Quinton's fair skin glowed with color. With slow deliberation she set the glass down on the table and crushed her cigarette out in the onyx tray.

"I really don't have to tell you you're an arrogant bastard after all," she said clearly. "You know what you are—and you enjoy it."

"I'll call a taxi for you." Jord's voice was bland.

"Don't bother," she retorted heatedly. "I'm sure the doorman can do that." She lifted her chin to face him. "I'd rather wait down there than force another minute of my unwanted presence on you. No, don't get up. I'll find my coat and see myself out."

In a silence louder than thunder she got out of the chair and walked gracefully across the room to climb the steps. Jord watched her, his eyes narrowed. When the door clicked shut, telling them that she was gone, Brad let his breath out in a long whistle.

Jord turned toward him, not a trace of regret flickering in his eyes. "Do you have the number of subscribers for the month of August?"

It was a cool dismissal that left Brad chilled. Jord had put the episode with Carol Quinton out of his mind the moment she walked out the door—or so Brad thought. But later, when Jord picked up the receiver of the phone and punched out a long-distance number, he drawled, "I decided I needed some fresh country air."

Into the phone he said, "Margie? I'm going to take you up on that invitation."

Brad couldn't understand the woman's answer, but he could hear the excited quality of her tone echoing in the receiver. His own spirits fell; he hadn't believed Jord would actually go through with it. But evidently the Quinton woman had tipped the scales.

Jord concluded the conversation and rang off.

In one last desperate attempt to make Jord see reason Brad straightened in the chair and tried to marshal his arguments. When he thought he had them together, he said, "You can't be seriously considering traveling all that way to attend the birthday party of your cousin's child."

Jord turned cool brown eyes to him. "Jamie isn't my cousin's child."

Brad stared at him. "Then—who is he?"

"The boy bears my name."

"You mean he's your son?" His head reeling, Brad lost sight of all his carefully worked out arguments.

Jord hesitated. "Legally—yes."

Brad sat in stunned silence. "I didn't even know you were married." He shook his head. "And your cousin is raising your child?"

Jord's eyes narrowed. "No. He stays with his grandmother. But the woman who is really rearing him is his aunt, my former wife's sister, Trisha Flannery."

CHAPTER TWO

A month later, under a broiling July sun, Trisha steered the ancient pickup down the dusty main street of Arien, a frown lining the smooth skin between the fine, dark brows. She felt hot and sticky with perspiration, and the wriggling boy on the car seat beside her didn't help her frame of mind. "Jamie, please be still and help me look for Irner."

"Why do I have to help you look for Irner?" Dark-brown eyes looked out from under silky blond lashes, their long length slightly darker closer to the lid. Her nephew was already a handsome boy.

"Because we need him to help us fix the baler," she said with an exasperated impatience that was barely contained. With a twist of the wheel she pulled into a parking space. Dark-blue eyes scanned the few buildings in front of her, a bank, a café, a bar and grill. In the last ten years Arien had shrunk from its already meager size to something less than a small town and was beginning to take on the look of an abandoned mining camp. The dry weather added to its sense of desolation. Hot air hung heavily over the two-block town; the whole atmosphere was oppressive.

There was a prediction that the July drought was going to

break, and it was that prediction that made Trisha's errand all the more urgent. She had half a field of hay cut and still lying on the ground and a recalcitrant baler that, after working well all morning, suddenly refused to tie the twine on a single bale. She got out of the car, her tall, slender body in faded denim shorts and a cotton shirt open at her throat. She straightened and scanned the sky. Heavy, thick white thunderclouds loomed against blue in the north. She might have two hours yet, if she was lucky. And on top of her fight with the baler and her race with the weather, she had promised to help Margie and her mother set tables at the hall tonight.

The slam of the other car door brought her out of her unhappy, muddled thoughts. Jamie had gotten out and was standing beside her, his small body dancing up and down with an eagerness to cross the street. "Come on," she said to him. "Let's try George's."

Jamie's face lit up with delight. He was rarely allowed in that place of mysterious adult activity.

The bar and grill was cool with air-conditioning, and for a moment Trisha had a wild urge to simply sit down in one of the old-fashioned leather booths, order a soda for Jamie and a cool drink for herself, and forget, for just a few minutes, that she had foolishly taken on the task of farming a half-section of land after her stepfather died so that she and her mother could remain on the farm that had been in their family for generations. But she couldn't forget. She had to get that hay into the barn before the coming rain.

Irner was there, nursing a glass of ale. He frowned when he saw her, and inwardly she heaved a sigh. She had learned to do minor repairs, but when she had examined the baler this afternoon, she had seen that a major welding job was required. Irner looked cool and comfortable perched on the stool in front of the curved bar, and he would not relish going out into the heat and working on her old, run-down equipment. He had told her the last time he'd repaired it that it was a heap of junk and she ought to take it to the scrap dealer and get what she could for the old iron in it. No one else used old equipment like that, he'd told her scornfully. These days everybody hired the big commercial balers to come in and do the job quickly and efficiently. She hadn't answered him, but she was sure he guessed she couldn't afford to pay the fee for a commercial baler. Even with the cost of repairs she saved a substantial sum of money by nursing the old baler through each season.

Irner half-turned and leaned an elbow on the bar with an air of resignation. He was in his sixties, his face lined, his skin leathery. Sometimes when Trisha saw him, she was reminded of a small, wizened monkey with bright eyes that couldn't hide a sharp intelligence.

"I somehow had a feeling I'd see you before this day was over," he drawled.

"Now why would you think a thing like that?" She lifted her chin and chided him with the half-kidding tone she knew he wanted to hear. Irner had known her all her life, and he treated her with the indulgent disdain of an old uncle. He wasn't satisfied unless he thought he'd managed to rouse a flash of her Irish temper.

"Tom Forrest came in this morning and said he'd driven by and seen you out baling hay."

"Tom Forrest ought to get a job with the Emmetsburg *Reporter*," she countered.

"Him and me both." The corner of his thin lips lifting, Irner heaved an exaggerated sigh. "Anything would be better than what I do—running at the beck and call of the female farmer in the district . . ."

"Well, would you mind 'running' a little faster?" Trisha mocked. "I've got half a field to finish up, and that rain's not going to hold off much longer."

He gave her a long-suffering look. "Guess it must be true there's no rest for the wicked." He lifted the glass of ale to his lips and drained it in several long swallows. Jamie watched the man's Adam's apple move, his brown eyes wide with fascination.

Irner lowered the heavy glass to the bar and wiped his mouth with the back of his hand. A grin split his lips as he looked down at the young boy. "What's the matter, son? Couldn't you fix that baler for your aunt like you did the last time?"

Jamie shook his head. "No. It's too hard. You have to do it."

The man slid off the stool, brushed his hand against the boy's ear, and produced a wrapped red-and-white peppermint round. Even Trisha, after watching him for years, never caught him palming the candy.

"You'd probably work a sight better without this candy in your ear."

Jamie's eyes sparkled. "Gee, thanks." His small hand clutched the sweet. "How do you do that, anyway?"

"Learned it when I joined the welder's union," Irner said mock-soberly, clapping the boy on the shoulder and guiding him toward the door.

At Irner's invitation and Jamie's insistence she gave the boy permission to ride with Irner in his truck. She stood on the sidewalk and watched while Irner boosted the boy up to the door handle of the ancient black cab so that he could open it himself. When he had succeeded in yanking it open, Jamie sent her back a melting grin and with Irner's help scrambled into the truck.

She turned away, thinking she was very lucky. Everyone in the community doted on the boy. Jamie didn't have one father—he had dozens. But only last night, with the excitement of Jord's visit, he had asked about his father again. It was getting harder to give him vague answers that wouldn't arouse his curiosity all the more.

Trisha's hands clenched. She walked across the sidewalk, her mind totally absorbed with her hatred. He was a devil, a monster, a big-city executive who had spent so many summers in Iowa they had forgotten he didn't live by their values. He took what he wanted. He used people, coldly, unfeelingly. He had

34

married her sister, and when she became pregnant, he had asked for a divorce.

She could forgive him for falling under the spell of her sister's potent charm, she could even forgive him for wanting to possess her beautiful body—but she couldn't forgive him his callous disregard for his son.

Is that what you can't forgive him for, her mind whispered, *or do you hate him because he married your beautiful sister instead of you?*

She reached for the pickup door and opened it with a violent thrust, almost knocking down the man she hadn't seen beside it.

"Hey." Judson Adams, Margie's husband, Jord's cousin, laughed at her and gingerly stepped away from the side of the vehicle door. "Come back to earth with the rest of us." He lifted his hand and smoothed the furrowed line on her forehead with a fingertip. "Nothing can be that bad."

Her stepbrother's affectionate gesture startled and disturbed her—disturbed her almost as much as the sight of his tall, lean body planted directly in front of her. She drew back slightly, and his brown eyes gleamed as if he knew exactly what she was thinking. His hand dropped away from her face, and his smile faded.

She felt compelled to explain. "I—didn't see you. You frightened me." Out of the corner of her eye she caught a glimpse of the orange Omni, covered with a coat of country dust. Judson must have pulled in, parked, and climbed out while she was too deep in thought to notice.

He smiled a slow smile, and that lazy lift of his lips made a strange tremor ripple through her. The sun gleamed down on his hair, bleached a bright gold by the sun. His throat and arms were exposed by the open collar and rolled-up sleeves of the denim shirt he wore, his skin tanned a deep bronze from his work out in the field. He was an attractive male, and his physical likeness to Jord still had the power to haunt her. "That was obvious." He smiled. "Having trouble with the baler again?"

35

She gave him a rueful glance. "How did you know?"

"I saw Jamie getting the royal treatment from Irner." Judson shook his head. "I can't believe he still drives the old relic that I used to love riding in when I was a kid." He stared down the street, gazing at the dust cloud that still lingered after Irner's departure, a reflective look on his face.

"Yes, he loves to ride in Irner's truck—just like every other kid in this county." She made a restless move, hoping that Judson would take the hint and allow her to pass by him and climb into her pickup. "Well, I'd better get going if I'm going to get that hay in—"

He caught her arm, his fingers biting into her flesh. Her eyes flew up to his face. It was cool, emotionless. "Have you thought any more about our adopting him?"

She stared at him. "Judson, you know it isn't up to me."

He said, "But you are the one who's borne the major burden of his upbringing, and naturally Marge and I are concerned about your feelings. But we've got to think about Jamie, too. If Marge and I adopted him, he'd have two parents—not just one. And you'd be free to get married and start a family of your own."

Her eyes flashed. "If I wanted to get married, I would. Having Jamie wouldn't stop me."

She moved as if to break away from his hold, but Judson's grip tightened. "All right, all right, so that wasn't a good argument." Judson's eyes held hers. "I should have known it wouldn't do to try to appeal to you on a selfish level." He smiled disarmingly. "I'm not saying you haven't done an excellent job with the boy. You have, and I didn't mean to imply otherwise. There's no question about how he'll turn out. But can't you consider it for Margie's sake? You know how much she loves Jamie. She sees him as a substitute for that baby she lost. Our—little girl would have been six this year." His voice roughened. "We've waited so long—and now we probably aren't going to be able to get a child from a regular adoption agency after all. There just aren't any to be had."

Trisha met his gaze steadily. "I'm sorry, Judson. Truly I am. But I just don't see how you can expect me to hand Jamie over to you and then turn my back on him—as if he didn't exist—"

Judson's amiability fell away. "Dammit, I'm not asking you to do that. I'm asking you to let me adopt him legally. You haven't even been able to do that. What if his father comes back and decides to claim him?"

"He won't," Trisha said shortly. "He hasn't tried to collect Jamie in five years—why would he do it now?"

"Because the boy is older. He isn't a baby anymore. Dammit, Trisha, don't you see that I"—he stopped, and in the heat he lifted a hand to his perspiring forehead—"that is, Margie and I would be in a better position to fight Deverone than you and your mother are?"

"No, I don't see that at all." She reached out to open the door of the pickup. "And if you think I'd hand Jamie over to that swine without a fight, you're mistaken. Jud, I'm sorry—I've got to go. I've got a hay crop to take care of."

Reluctance in every line of his body, he dropped his hand from her arm and stepped away. "I won't give up, you know."

"You'd need permission from Jord to adopt him. And somehow, even though he never comes near the boy, I think he'd refuse."

"We wouldn't know until we tried," Judson said quietly, his eyes fastened on her face. "Margie is a favorite of his—he's always been fond of her."

Trisha shook her head, her frown returning. "I don't think that would make any difference. Right now it would be best to let sleeping dogs lie."

She turned to climb into the pickup, but Judson's hand on the window after she was seated inside stopped her from starting the motor. "Sure you don't need help this afternoon? I could spare you some time."

She shook her head. "I'll manage."

An understanding smile played over his lips. "Okay, tough lady. I know when I'm being told to go mind my own business."

She laughed and started the engine, pulling out of the parking space with a roar and throwing a wave to him out the window as she drove away.

She bumped over the gravel road, thinking about her conversation with Judson. She wished Judson would stop talking to her about adopting Jamie. He was like a bulldog, getting a grip on her and hanging on. Jamie was hers, and he always would be. Trisha's hands clenched the wheel in unconscious determination. Suddenly from nowhere came the unbidden thought, *But why are you so determined to keep the boy? Is it because you were once in love with his father—and when you look at Jamie, you think of him?*

A violent forward movement of her foot on the brake halted the pickup, and she made the turn from the road into the narrow lane. But nothing, no physical action could make her forget the fact that she had fallen in love with her sister's lover, that Jord Deverone had fished her out of the lake one night and held her cold and nearly naked body close to his warm one and told her how beautiful she was . . . she wheeled over the slight rise and pulled into the yard, nearly running headlong into the back of Irner's truck, parked in front of the house. That was the second time in the space of a day she had nearly run into something because she was thinking about Jord Deverone. Her confrontation with Judson had triggered these thoughts, but she would curb them, she must. There was no future in thinking about Jamie's father. Jamie was her life now—and her responsibility, no matter what Judson Adams might say.

Irner, wearing a protective helmet and face shield, was already working on the baler, a blue flame rising from his welder. Jamie had been positioned a careful distance away by the man, Trisha was sure, but now he was edging closer.

"Get back," she warned him sharply. Jamie jumped backward, his blond hair nearly standing on end with surprise. Trisha rarely spoke to him with such a sharp edge in her voice, and he hadn't seen her walk across the yard.

After another ten minutes Irner raised the visor on the protective helmet and grumbled, "Well, that should hold you for this afternoon. Doubt if it will last through the fall season, though. You've got to get rid of this old baler, Trish."

"I know. Maybe I will—next year, when my ship comes in." Her depression vanished with the knowledge that she had a good chance to beat the rain, and she swung up on the tractor and sat down in the dish seat, Jamie scrambling after her. "Thanks, Irner. Send me the bill."

"Oh, I will," he assured her and went on talking and shaking his head, but his words were lost in the roar of the Allis-Chalmers as the tractor came to life. She pulled down the throttle, tossed a quick wave to Irner over her shoulder, checked to see that Jamie was firmly seated in the special place she had made for him, and let out the clutch. "Go fast," he urged, and she obeyed, making the hay wagon that trailed after the baler rattle along with a loud bumping that made any further conversation impossible.

Ominous rumblings in the sky told her she wasn't driving fast enough. To make matters worse, she hadn't made the frequent stops that were required to stack the bales as they came out of the baler and spilled automatically onto the flat wagon. They were jumbled in a precarious heap at the end of the baler, and if she didn't stop soon and rearrange them, they'd tumble to the ground, and she'd end up with the infinitely more difficult task of hoisting several of the forty-pound bales back up onto the flat trailer.

Stopping at the crest of the hill, she gritted her teeth, put the tractor in neutral, and briefly indulged in the fantasy that Jamie was a strapping sixteen-year-old. But he wasn't. With a small sigh she jumped down from the tractor and walked across the hay stubble to hop up onto the trailer. A thunder clap banged almost directly over her head, and with a force born of desperation she began pushing the bales around, shoving them into place, rolling one over the other in a kind of half-carry, half-push that she had perfected over the years. The prickly dry leaves from the hay showered her bare arms and legs.

"Aunt Trish." Jamie was shouting above the noise of the tractor. "Look. Somebody's in our yard."

She shoved another bale into place and turned to follow the line of Jamie's pointing finger. From the rise of the hill where she had stopped, she could see that a sleek gray car stood just in front of the doorstep.

With a vicious softness she swore under her breath. She didn't have the remotest idea who her caller could be, and she didn't particularly care. It was probably just a salesman, and he should know better than to come in the middle of the afternoon in haying season, anyway.

Another rumble of thunder reached her ears. She turned her back and began her task again, knowing that whoever it was would simply have to go away and come back later.

Satisfied in another moment that she had stacked the bales well enough to ensure their staying on the wagon, she had pivoted to jump to the ground when she saw the silver-gray car make a wide circle and drive out of the yard. Shrugging, she got back on the tractor and was engaging the clutch when Jamie said, "Look. Someone's driving our pickup away."

With a grimace she remembered leaving the keys in the ignition. She often did during the daytime. She had never dreamed anyone would want that old relic, and incidents of car stealing in this part of the country were minimal, anyway. But now it was evident that someone had discovered her carelessness and was driving away with her one mode of transportation. "No—" She flew down off the tractor and had begun to run, not exactly sure what she would do, when she heard Jamie shout, "It's coming this way."

Stunned, she stumbled to a halt and stood watching in disbelief as the pickup rattled along the path toward the hayfield.

Expertly the driver wheeled the vehicle around the corner and directed it on a course that sent it bouncing across the stubble. It was then that she caught a glimpse of the driver, and every nerve in her body tensed. It was a man. His features were concealed by the glare of light off the windshield, but she could see his hair was wheat colored, a slightly darker shade than Jamie's. A cool breeze from the coming thunderstorm lifted her dark hair and threaded it across her throat. She brushed it away, intensely aware of the shiver of emotion that was holding her rooted to the spot. A remembered sensation of fear and excitement sang through her, making her nerves quiver with wild fury.

A few feet from the hay wagon the pickup ground to a halt. The door opened—and the man she had never wanted to see again as long as she lived stepped out of the cab.

Her first stupidly inconsequential thought was: *My God, I'd forgotten how tall he is! And how male!* His tall, lean frame was clad in snug-fitting blue denims and a short-sleeved knit shirt that lay partially open at the throat and exposed a curious mixture of brown and golden hairs in its hollow. The short sleeves exposed his tanned arms. Long, tautly muscled thighs propelled him easily over the rolling terrain as if he had lived in the country all his life. But he hadn't. . . .. He stopped just in front of her, and the aura of power and virility that surrounded him seemed to reach out and grasp her by the throat.

"Hello, Trisha." Brown eyes the color and texture of stones moved over her heated face, seemed almost to touch the breasts straining against the cotton blouse tied up under her midriff, flickered down the length of golden thigh her too-short cutoffs exposed.

"What are you doing here?" Her head whirled. Had the heat created the hateful image of Jord Deverone out of her thoughts? No, she wasn't dreaming. She could almost feel Jamie's intent interest behind her and the drone of the tractor as it ground on, uselessly burning fuel.

Softly he said the words that had haunted her subconscious dreams for years. "I came to see—Jamie."

Like a female tiger ready to protect her cub, she tensed and clenched her fists. "You're too late," she rasped, "about five years too late. He belongs to me."

A loud clap of thunder followed her defiant statement. He glanced up at the sky, and a frown tightened his brows. Before she could move or speak, he said, "Let's get this hay in. Then we'll talk about it." He bent and pulled his shirt off, rolling it up into a ball and tossing it onto the highest bale, where it would be out of the way. The sight of his broad shoulders and the light covering of blond hair over his chest made her throat fill.

"Get off my land, Deverone." To her horror her voice shook.

"Don't be a fool. Get that tractor moving." Hard command simmered in his voice.

He climbed lithely onto the wagon and stood up, planting his feet, readying himself for the forward movement of the tractor. She glared up at him, hating his male assurance, hating the sight of him. But when the thunder rumbled again and he ordered roughly, "Get a move on, dammit," she ducked her head and ran to the tractor.

She could drive faster now with Jord on the back, receiving the bales that were dumped out of the baler. She pushed the throttle ahead and concentrated on watching the baler teeth rake up and devour the cut swath of hay.

"Who is he, Aunt Trish?" Jamie shouted above the noise of the tractor.

"Just somebody who came to help," she lied and went back to watching the row, her heart pounding with fear. If Jord had finally decided to claim Jamie, how could she stop him? He had everything on his side, money, power, influence. He would turn a deaf ear to her arguments that Jamie had spent all his life with her, that he would be puzzled and lonely if he were taken from her. She was his mother, in actuality, if not biologically. The only

42

other people he claimed as his own were Margie and her mother and Judson. If Judson could get legal help for her—

Thoughts raced around inside her head like caged animals. Did she have the right to think only of herself? What about Jamie? What about the things Jord could offer him, a college education, an entree into a type of society she could only read about in magazines? Did she have the right to come between the boy and his father? But suppose Jord's interest in Jamie was as fleeting as his interest in Diane had been . . .

The thunder and the lightning were very close now, and she only wanted to get Jamie away from danger. The last swath of hay disappeared inside the baler. She looked back at Jord only to be tormented by the sight of his naked back bent over a bale. Muscles rippled under skin satiny with perspiration as he strained to lift the last one in place. She swiveled her head violently around to the front and pushed the throttle open wider. Her increased speed would give him a very bumpy ride, but she didn't care. Why should she show him any consideration? He had never shown any for Diane.

She had nearly reached the barn when the heavens opened. She pulled the tractor to a stop and shouted to Jamie, "Run to the house. I've got to get the tarp over the hay."

Jamie obeyed instantly, hopping down off the tractor and scooting across the grassy yard. The rain poured over her face and soaked her clothes, but she ignored it and ran to the barn. She supposed Jord was getting soaked, too, but she couldn't have cared less. Inside she hurried past Black Prince, the Arab gelding who was bumping his stall in nervous reaction to the storm.

"Shush, baby, it's all right. You're okay." The tarp lay loosely folded in a heap in the next stall. She grabbed it and dragged it back past Black Prince and out into the deluge.

She almost ran into him. He had evidently been coming to see what she was doing. Now he grasped the other corner of the tarp and nearly pulled her off her feet as he jogged toward the trailer with it.

43

He jumped up on the bales, dragging the end of the tarp with him. She did the same, and together, despite the rain pouring over them, they managed to get the hay covered and the wet strings of the tarp tied to the end posts of the wagon. Just as they were finishing, a crack of lightning hit a tree on the other side of the barn and sent it crashing to the earth. Trisha jumped and cried out, and Jord said a succinct word and grabbed her. He manhandled her off the wagon and strode to the barn, towing her along beside him like so much excess baggage.

The door was cut in half, Dutch fashion, and he reached inside and slipped the hook out of the eye and thrust her through. He followed and closed the door behind him.

In the half-dark shelter of the barn fragrant with the smell of hay and horse, her nerves jangled with primitive awareness of the man whose hand still gripped her arm. As if sensing her awareness, he turned her toward him. In the light from the open top half of the door, she could see him far too well. He loomed beside her like a primitive man from a primeval rain forest, his body an inviting contrast of textures, his shoulders silky with moisture, golden body hair crisp and curling, hard muscles sheathed under sleek skin. A wild and wanton need to touch him burned inside her. She was mesmerized, bewitched, unable to move. He was casting a spell over her in this dark and shadowed barn, his silken tentacles tightening slowly around her. He was possessing her with nothing more than the flicker of his lazy gaze, almost touching her with his eyes as they wandered over her face, down to the patch of bare, wet skin at her waist exposed by her midriff-tied blouse, and lower to the curve of her slender thighs. When he had taken his fill of the long length of her, his eyes returned to linger boldly on the taut, wet fabric that covered her breasts. She stood utterly still, knowing that she wanted his eyes on her, knowing that she wanted to touch and be touched, kiss and be kissed. Oh, God, this was insanity. How could she still want him to make love to her after what he had done?

44

"Let go of me." The voice that should have been coldly cutting was husky and shaking.

"No," he said huskily. "Not this time . . ."

He grasped her other arm and slowly pulled her closer. Instinctively she put her hands on his chest to fend him off. Her palms came in contact with his nipples, and she gasped and snatched her fingers away as if she had been burned.

He rasped, "Don't pretend you don't enjoy touching me. Put your hands on me, Trisha. Admit that I exist—and that you want me . . ."

His hands on her upper arms were bringing her inexorably closer. "I don't want you," she whispered. "I hate everything about you, your arrogance, your selfishness, your money—"

"But you don't hate my body, do you? Right now you're loving it with your eyes, just as I'm loving yours—"

Like a tiger playing with its prey, he had tolerantly allowed her to maintain her distance. Now hard arms wrapped themselves around her, and his head bent to hers. In that instant before their mouths met, the rain drummed on the roof and her heart accelerated to match its primitive cadence.

Then his lips closed over hers, warm and male and demanding. His possession of her mouth was followed by the thrusting entrance of his tongue. A shuddering sense of belonging, of rightness shivered through her to a sensual core. Her hands went of their own accord to his back and telegraphed their disturbing message of cool, sleek skin. Her clothes seemed an unwelcome barrier between their moist bodies. She arched her back to press her breasts against his chest, seeking the erotic pleasure she remembered from a million dreams. The muscles of his thighs and legs were hard and corded against the softness of hers.

He went on kissing her, and she tilted her head to give him greater access to every corner of her mouth. A soft groan reached her ears. His hands shaped themselves to her back, finding the bare skin of her midriff, moving up under the cloth. Then, inexplicably, he emitted another soft groan, loosened his grip, and lessened the pressure on her mouth. Knowing he was going to end the kiss, she gave a soft incoherent moan of distress and clutched at him, unwilling to let him take away the heaven he was giving her. He acceded to her demands, and when he had taken his pleasure of her mouth once more, he lifted his head to look at her, his eyes gleaming with triumph. "Trisha. Dear God. I never thought you'd accept me so quickly, forgive me so much . . ."

His words were like the voice of the serpent in her dream of Eden. She thrust him away, and because he had not expected it, she caught him off balance. She stepped free of his embrace and whipped her anger to a raging fury. "Forgive you?" Her voice was hoarse with contempt. "I'll never forgive you. I'll see you in hell before I'll forgive you for what you did to my sister."

"I did nothing to your sister," he said quietly, and somehow the calm answer infuriated her even more.

"No, you did nothing to my sister." Her voice was harsh with irony. "You only seduced her, made her pregnant, and then walked out on her and left her to raise your child alone."

Every vestige of the warmth and charm that had been there a moment ago left his face. "That's not true," he said huskily.

The blatant lie made her temper explode out of the top of her head. "It is," she cried, "it's true, and I'll never forgive you, never—"

She turned to run out of the barn, but he caught her upper arms and pulled her around to face him, forcing her against the cold, cement-block wall. "No," he said implacably. "The thing you can't forgive me for is this—"

He gripped her hair and held her head still for the downward swoop of his mouth. But when his lips touched ..ers, there was no longer any cruelty in his embrace. His mouth was warm and possessive, tender and persuasive. His hands pulled her away from the wall, and he spread his palm over the sensitive hollow of her lower back, pressing her against him, making her aware of his masculine arousal and the way their tall bodies fit together as if they had been made for each other. All thought of resistance fled, and she let her hands rediscover his cool, wet back.

He moved as if to end the kiss, and unconsciously her hands flexed to hold him. He made a small sound of satisfaction and lifted his head. Holding her, he smiled a slow, mocking smile, his eyes gleaming with triumph. "That," he said softly, "is why you hate me."

Shuddering with the cold knowledge that he was right, she met his gaze, her blue eyes like steel, her hands on his chest, pushing. "Let go of me."

"No—"

Desperate to get out of his arms, she used the one weapon she had against him. "Let go of me, damn you. I've got to go see about Jamie."

His hands fell away, and she whirled around. After a moment's fumbling with the catch on the door she was free, walking across the wet grass in the pouring rain.

He followed her, and together they made their way across the yard to the house. Oh, God, she thought desperately, how could she have succumbed to his kisses? How could she have responded to him like that? She had practically begged him to go on kissing her. He had made one move toward her, and she had fallen into his arms. How could she have kissed him so wantonly? Every movement of her mouth and body had been an open invitation for him to go on making love to her. . . .

The rain had lessened, but she wished it was still raining torrents. She wished she could stand in the cleansing downpour and wash away the feel of him from her body, the scent of him from her nose. She couldn't love him. He was a worthless, roving womanizer, a man totally without scruples, but she had fallen for his practiced charm with little or no resistance. She was a traitor to her sister, a traitor to Jamie . . . Jamie!

She wrenched open the door, and in the shelter of awning that covered the back-porch door she stopped short and turned. Only his catlike reflexes kept him from stumbling over her. "You can't come in," she told him coolly.

"Watch me." Cool brown eyes challenged her to stop him.

In desperation she said, "If you try to take Jamie from me, I'll fight you with everything I've got."

He turned to glance behind him at the unpainted buildings, the unkempt state of the yard. His gaze ended on the ancient baler. "Which isn't much—is it?"

His cool assessment of her financial state fanned the flames of her anger to a newer, hotter blaze. "Whatever it takes to stop you," she ground out, "I'll use it. I'll drag you into court—here, where the judge will be sympathetic to my case."

A hard impatience thinned his mouth. "I haven't come to take Jamie away from you."

A sharp gasp escaped her, followed by a play of disbelief across her features. "You haven't?"

"No. I merely came to see him."

Her feeling of relief was tempered with a sharp, contrary anger. "No," she said, her voice scathing. "I should have known better. You would never want Jamie with you. He might get in the way of your jet-setting life, your nights with your women."

A hard, sardonic smile lifted his mouth. "Did anyone ever tell you you're a very perverse woman? When you thought I wanted Jamie, you were ready to fight me tooth and claw. Now you're accusing me of a selfish lack of interest in him."

"I'd have more respect for you if you demanded to have him back and took me to court. At least then I'd believe you were willing to accept your obligation as a father—even though you walked out on your wife."

His face darkened. "I accepted my obligations to Diane in exactly the way she wanted."

"You deserted her." The words hung in the air.

Jord gave her a dark, hooded look. "How did you come to that conclusion?"

"You left her just when she needed you most."

48

Her words made the color drain away from his face. Then he said harshly, "She told you that?"

"She didn't have to! She had to come home to have her baby—"

He shook his head. "We married, agreeing to stay together for six months, that's all. After that we would separate for a period of time and then get a divorce. Diane wanted her freedom."

"She couldn't have."

"*Dammit, it was her idea!* She didn't want me around when Jamie was born."

"She must have," Trisha cried. "Jamie is your son—"

"Is he?" The two words were heavy with denial.

Every drop of color drained from her face. "My God! You can't actually be denying it. Jamie is living proof. He looks like you—he even acts like you."

He said nothing. She stared at him, her violet eyes wide, her face pale with rage. "Oh, my God. Don't. Don't try to lie about Jamie on top of everything else."

"All right," he said, his face bleak. "I won't try to explain it all to you tonight. But sooner or later, Trisha Flannery, you'll hear the truth from me, and trust me enough to believe it. Now are you going to open the door and let me come in and get dried off—or are we going to stand in the porch all night?"

The door that separated the porch from the house swung open. Jamie stood inside, his favorite Big Bird pajama tops buttoned all wrong, his legs bare below the short yellow pants, the familiar wheat-colored cowlick standing up at the back of his head. "Are you coming in? I don't want to be alone anymore. I'm scared."

Trisha bent over and put a protective arm over the boy's shoulders, shepherding him away from the cool draft coming in the door. "Yes, honey. Right away."

Jord Deverone followed. She shot him a heated look over her shoulder as he shut the door behind him, but she was reluctant to upset Jamie by bluntly telling him to get out of the house.

Jamie's sturdy little body felt trembly under her hands. He'd had enough fright for one evening. She couldn't risk upsetting him even more. He was a sensitive child—unlike his father.

Jamie was used to being left in the house for short periods while she was out in the field, and he had turned on the light in the big kitchen. An empty, milk-stained glass by the sink was evidence that he had poured himself a glass of milk. But she was sure he was starved. The candy Irner had given him was a poor substitute for the afternoon snack she usually gave the boy, milk and a piece of cake, or home-baked bread with her own strawberry jelly inches deep and dripping off the sides. Now there was the immediate task of feeding him his supper and getting him to bed. It had been a long, exhausting day for both of them, with several disturbing events, not the least of which was Jord Deverone's intrusion into their lives. Even now Jamie was turning wide brown eyes up to the man who stood half-naked beside his aunt. Curiosity was written all over his face. She knew it would be better to introduce Jord to him at once than to try to answer Jamie's questions.

"This is—Jord, honey. He came to—to visit the farm."

"And to see you," Jord told Jamie softly, making Trisha bristle.

"Why would you want to see me?" Jamie was plainly puzzled.

"I heard you're having a birthday soon," Jord said easily, "and I wanted to see your cake."

"Aunt Marge is fixing it for me," he said earnestly. "Are you coming to my party?"

"I think so," Jord replied, his eyes glittering at the wicked darts Trisha was sending from hers. "I got a special invitation."

Jamie climbed up on the utility stool Trisha kept for him next to the counter and squirmed around to face Jord. "A special invitation?"

Jord nodded. "From your Aunt Marge. By telephone. She called all the way out to New York, where I live, and asked me to come."

50

"Why would she do that?" Jamie tilted his head and eyed Jord quizzically. Trisha shot him a hot, angry look. *Yes, Mr. Big Shot, answer that one! Why would she do that?*

Jord didn't miss a beat. "Because she knows you're very special to me."

"I'm not special to anybody except Grandma and Aunt Trisha and Aunt Marge and Uncle Jud. They're the only ones I'm special to."

Trisha couldn't keep the glitter of triumph from her eyes. Jord frowned, and the boy stared back at Jord owlishly. Unable to stop herself, Trisha chided softly, out of Jamie's earshot, "You see? I told you he was like you."

Jord's frown deepened. He made an exasperated sound and then said, "Would it be possible for me to get out of these wet clothes?"

Now it was her turn to frown. Then, after a moment of thought, she said curtly, "I kept a few things that belonged to Simon. You'll find his robe hanging in the north bedroom if you'd like to change. Bring your jeans down, and I'll put them in the dryer. I suppose since you'll have to stay until your clothes dry, you might as well share an omelet with us."

"Your hospitality overwhelms me," he muttered in her ear.

"You did invite yourself," she shot back and felt as if she had scored a minor victory when he grimaced and went around the corner to the stairwell. She would wait to change out of her own wet clothes until Jord came down.

Jamie's inquisitive eyes studied Trisha's face. "How does he know where everything is?"

"He used to come here every summer and stay with your Uncle Judson's father," Trisha explained in an offhanded way. "And he came here often to see—your mother." She went to the refrigerator and took out half a dozen eggs. She supposed Jord would be hungry.

Jamie's eyes lit up. "He knew my mother?"

"Yes." Trisha set her burden on the counter, took a bowl

down from the cabinet, and picked up an egg to give it a hard crack against the side.

Jamie heaved a sigh. "I wish I had knowed her."

"Known, honey."

"Known," he repeated dutifully. Childlike, his mind reverted quickly to the present. "What are you making?"

"An omelet."

"Can we have biscuits?"

"Yes, sure." There was a noise from upstairs that sounded suspiciously like the clunk of a man's pants falling to the floor. Her nerves quivered. She beat the eggs with a nervous energy, wielding the wire whip vigorously in the bowl.

Jamie slid down from the chair. "Can I get the biscuit mix out, please?"

"Yes, of course. And how'd you like to be my handyman and get that omelet pan from lower left shelf of that bottom cabinet?"

Jamie put the bright yellow box of mix on the counter and was crawling halfway into the cupboard in search of the pan when a male voice said, "I'll take these down to the basement and dry them if I may."

She jumped and gasped. Jamie scrambled out of the cupboard and stared at her. "What's wrong?" he asked, his little-boy concern for her making her heart turn over.

Before she could answer, Jord said quietly, "I must have frightened her, son."

The sound of Jord's low voice calling Jamie his son made her heart do another annoying flip-flop. She turned to find him staring at her and Jamie both with a strange gleam in his eyes.

"I'll take your clothes down," she said crisply and held out her hand.

"I'll watch the boy while you go and change," he returned easily.

His eyes moved over her, and she was suddenly and uncomfortably aware that the wet clothes she wore were clinging to her damp skin.

"I'll take you up on that offer."

Minutes later, when she returned to the kitchen feeling infinitely warmer and more secure in a pair of denim pants and a white sweater with a sunburst pattern of color at its neck, she discovered Jord standing over the stove, tall and disturbingly masculine, Simon's navy-blue silk robe belted around his waist, the hem barely brushing the tops of his knees. The smell of an omelet already browning reached her nose.

Knowing he wore nothing under that thin silk garment, for she had just put his denims and dark briefs in the dryer, she averted her eyes from him and looked at Jamie. He was perched on the stool beside Jord, his eyes like saucers, his fingers plunged into a bowl of sticky biscuit dough.

"Jord's letting me make the biscuits. He says men have to learn to cook, too," Jamie told her, his brown eyes flying to her face, anxiously searching for signs of displeasure.

"He's absolutely right, little one. But did he also tell you it's bad for the biscuits to be kneaded too long?" She took the bowl from him and handed him a damp cloth for his sticky fingers.

Obediently Jamie began wiping his hands. "He just read the directions on the box. He says he doesn't know much about biscuits."

"I'm sure he's right about that," she said dryly, glad her back was to Jord as she added more flour to the mixture and turned it out on a board.

Deftly she rolled the dough into a flat rectangle and cut it with an inverted water glass. Jamie hopped down off his stool and came over to help her place the biscuits on a cookie sheet. "Did you men remember to preheat the oven?" she asked as she turned and was forced to face Jord again.

"Yes, we did," he murmured, his eyes mocking her. "It's all ready."

She wasn't sure how she managed to set the little table in the breakfast nook and mix the orange juice that would give Jamie a nutritious drink. Every nerve in her body jangled with awareness of the tall, lean man who stood at the stove and watched her every move. Somehow she got everything ready on time, and she was rather pleased with the effect of the sunny yellow plates against the white cloth she had put on the round table. If it wasn't up to the standards of the fancy restaurants Jord Deverone frequented, that was just too bad.

As if to mock her battle with the rain, the summer sun made a fleeting appearance. Painting the underside of the rain clouds with silver, a glorious sunset gleamed outside the window and filled the little nook with the pale glow of its last rays.

The omelet was rich with cheese and seasoned to tasty perfection. She was hungry after her struggle with the hay, and she couldn't hide her appreciation of the food Jord had cooked. He watched her fork the last bite into her mouth, his own mouth lifting in a smile as she give a little sigh of satisfaction. His eyes gleamed into hers with a silent, knowing look, as if he were reminding her that he could satisfy all her appetites. The thought made her flush with a quick anger and avert her eyes from that lazily relaxed, self-assured male across from her. Blissfully unaware of the crosscurrents between the two adults, Jamie munched on his third biscuit, strawberry jelly dripping over his fingers. When he had polished off the last bite, a sticky hand came up to his mouth to stifle a yawn. He slid closer to Trisha on the curved bench seat and rested his head on her shoulder.

"Tired, son?" Jord asked.

"No," he said and stifled another yawn.

"Why don't I take you up and tuck you in while your Aunt Trisha does the dishes?"

Trisha waited in a curious kind of suspension. Jamie had always insisted that she be the one to put him to bed. Young brown eyes met Jord's mature ones. "Because I'm special to you?"

"Yes, because you're special to me," Jord said with a warmth that disturbed Trisha.

Jamie sat very still on the bench, considering it. He wanted to say no, Trisha was sure, but he was reluctant to offend this tall stranger who had allowed him to put his fingers in the biscuit dough. "Okay," he said at last, his voice strangely adult. "You can tuck me in."

Trisha watched, wildly conflicting emotions running through her as Jamie slid past and stood outside the nook, waiting for Jord. She was afraid for Jamie, yet helpless to stop the budding relationship between him and his father. If Jamie should begin to look up to Jord with a hero-worship kind of devotion only to have Jord disappear out of his life, Jamie would be crushed. But she could hardly stop the boy's own father from talking to him.

Jord's face was coolly bland as he levered himself out of the curved seat and took the boy's hand. Jamie tilted his head to look up at the tall man who had reached out to grasp his hand, and Trisha felt her throat close with an unknown emotion. They left the room, and a need to dissipate her confused feelings made her jump to her feet and begin clearing the table with brisk movements.

She was nearly finished with the washing up when Jord came back into the kitchen. For a big man he could move with the quietness of a predatory cat, and he was almost beside her before she realized he was back in the room.

Her heart went back to its old acrobatic tricks, and defensively she said sharply, "Well? Did you have any trouble with him?"

"No." He was so close to her now that his breath caressed her cheek. "He washed his hands and went to bed without another word. He's a good boy—you've done a good job with him."

She gave her entire concentration to wiping around the rim of the sink and said nothing.

"It can't have been easy for you after my Uncle Simon died, raising the boy and keeping the farm going without him—"

Trisha tried not to wince. She still couldn't bear to be reminded that her stepfather was gone. The ache was still there. "We manage."

She faced him, her back to the sink that supported her sud-

55

denly uncooperative legs. She wanted him out of her house—and out of her life. "I'm sure your clothes are dry now. Where are you staying? I can take you in the pickup. I'm sure it isn't the kind of luxury vehicle you're used to, but—"

Anger flared in his eyes and then was damped down. "You know damn good and well I haven't spent my life riding around in Cadillacs."

She lifted her head, pride giving her tall body extra height. "But you do now. And that puts you right out of my category. You said you came to see Jamie. You've seen him. Now you can just go away, Mr. Deverone. Go back to the city where you came from."

"I'm not leaving until I accomplish what I came here to do." He didn't move closer. Then why did she feel as if he were touching her?

Her heart going like a trip-hammer, she forced herself to ask coolly, "If you haven't come to take Jamie away, then why did you come here?"

"I came to attend a birthday party." The soft words had a subtle, threatening tone that had nothing to do with their meaning. He moved closer, and quickly, before she could dodge away, he gripped the counter on both sides of her, trapping her within his muscular arms. She lifted her head and stared at him, defiant to the last. He whispered a word she couldn't understand, and bent his head, his mouth seeking and finding the sensitive spot at the base of her throat where her pulse pounded wildly.

"No—" Her protest was useless. His warm lips pleasured her and teased her skin till tingling excitement began its dizzy rise through her. "Please, Jord, oh, please—go away." All her defenses were gone, and her murmured words sounded more like a husky plea for him to continue rather than a request to stop.

CHAPTER THREE

He gathered her closer, his palm coming up to find the sweet, full curve of her breast. "Let me touch you. Let me free you from this prison we've both been locked in—"

"No—" Drowning, she clung to that one word as if it were a lifeline. If she could just keep saying no—

The telephone jangled, echoing shrilly in the big kitchen.

"Don't answer it," he murmured, moving his mouth over the long, dusky length of her eyelashes. "Let it ring."

"No—" With a surge of willpower she wrenched free from him. He let her go but stood watching her, his glittering eyes absorbing the movement of her breasts that betrayed her disturbed breathing. The telephone went again, and she tore free of his hypnotic gaze and walked to the phone that hung on the wall next to the stove.

It was Margie. Her cheerfulness seemed a remote and alien emotion projected into the tense atmosphere. Jord folded his arms and leaned back against the counter, his mouth tilted in a cynical smile. Her nervous system jangled in reaction. "Oh, you are home, then," Margie enthused in her ear. "I thought you were going to be here by seven. You're not having trouble with that ancient relic you drive, are you? I was afraid you might be stranded out on the road somewhere, and I was going to send Jud out looking for you if you didn't answer your telephone."

"No—" She took a deep breath and tried to marshal her thoughts. "No, I'm all right. I just—with the hay and the rain and all I forgot about going to the hall. I'm sorry."

"Oh, that's all right, don't worry about it. We've got most of the tables laid anyway. I was just worried about you, that's all. As long as I know you're all right, I can tell Mom. She was worried, too."

But she wasn't all right, not at all. She took a breath and said, "Jord is here."

There was a stunned little silence on the other end of the phone, and then Margie's breathless voice was asking, "What do you mean—here?"

"I mean here, in the house with me. He helped me with that last bit of hay. Would you like to talk to him?"

There was another beat of hesitation, and then she said quickly, "Yes, of course. Put him on, won't you?"

"Hello, sweetheart," he said warmly into the phone. "How are you?"

His voice changed completely when he talked to Margie. It always had. Margie, along with her mom, had earned his unwavering love and loyalty long ago.

Jord said, "Yes, I know Jamie's party isn't until next week, but I cleared away some things and decided to come a little earlier. Have I upset anyone's plans?"

He balanced the phone against his shoulder in a practiced way and turned to watch Trisha. No longer able to listen to his gentle tone or tolerate his eyes on her warm face, she left him and went into the living room, the room she had reserved for her evenings with Jamie, reading and watching TV. The colonial oval rug in shades of gold, rust, and cinnamon lay against the golden oak floor and provided a conversation circle bordered by the high-backed couch facing the television and two companion chairs on each side, all in coordinating colors of rust and soft green. There was ample space for Jamie to play and her to read her beloved art books. A twelve-room farmhouse built in the generous proportions of houses constructed after the Depression, it was too big for them. The house had seemed even bigger after Simon died. In the wintertime she closed off several rooms, but now, in the summer, she enjoyed every spacious inch. Cottonwoods grew protectively on three sides, and a cool evening breeze moved the chiffon curtain at the big double windows.

But the furniture was showing some wear on the arms, and there was a tear in the seam of the braided rug she hadn't gotten around to mending yet. Well, what of it? She was a working woman, and this was a farm. It wasn't meant to be a luxury condominium by the sea or an apartment in the old and exclusive Dakota building on Manhattan's Central Park, but it was home, the only one she had ever known—or ever would know. The land was paid for. All she had to do was meet the taxes each year and make enough to keep the farm going and support herself and Jamie and her mother.

She supposed that according to law Jord was responsible for some of the boy's support. But she had never asked for money—and he had never offered it. She didn't want his money. He was the last person she would ask for help.

Restlessly she sat down on the couch and picked up a magazine, knowing full well why she was looking at the house with critical and defensive eyes. She was comparing what she saw to her vision of what Jord's living quarters must be like—sophisticated and luxurious beyond anything, she was certain.

She clenched her teeth and flipped viciously through the brightly colored pages, seeing nothing on them. He was out of her realm. He had always been out of her realm. She had to remember that. She found an article about quilting that she thought might hold her interest, and determined to block the low, attractive rumble of Jord's voice out of her hearing, she began to read. But all too soon the conversation ended, and Jord was walking into the room. Uneasily she rose to her feet and faced him. "Are you ready to go now?"

It was then that she saw the coffee cup in his hand. Slowly he moved to the couch and eased himself down in the corner, carefully balancing his cup, the robe that was slightly too short for him falling away from his knees. "Your hospitality as a hostess leaves something to be desired." He stretched his long legs out in front of him. "I thought I might be allowed to drink a cup of coffee." He cocked his head as if listening for something and then expelled a long breath. "My God. I'd forgotten how quiet it is in the country."

"Don't get too comfortable, Mr. Deverone. You won't be here that long."

He turned to set his cup down on the table at the end of the couch and laid his head back on the high plaid cushion. The long lashes flickered down. "Ah, but that's where you're wrong, Miss Flannery. I'm not going anywhere."

"You can't stay here," she said sharply.

"Why not?" He didn't move a muscle. "You have plenty of room."

"You must have a place to stay somewhere. Who brought you? That car—"

"Was driven by my assistant, Brad Hunt."

"Well, call him. Have him come and get you—"

"No," he said softly. "He's taken a room in a motel in Emmetsburg, and I don't expect to see him again until he's finished with the three days' work he has ahead of him in preparation for a presentation I'm giving at the end of the month."

"Dandy," Trisha mocked. "I wish I had someone to do my work. How is he at hoeing cockleburs?"

His mouth quirked. "Not too good, I'm afraid."

"Jord, you simply can't stay here." She fought to keep her voice on an even keel. "The gossip would go through this community like wildfire."

A sudden hardness crossed the face that had been relaxed. "I don't give a damn anymore what this community thinks."

"But I do," Trisha said huskily. "You'll leave—but I'll have to go on living here."

He opened his eyes and turned his head to study her. "I promise you—your good name won't suffer."

The low intentness of his words radiated with male protectiveness and struck a resonant chord deep within her, a chord so deep and hidden her only coherent thought was to strike back. "Oh, you're very good at that, aren't you, Mr. Deverone? Protecting reputations, that's your strong suit."

She stared at him, her color high and brilliant, not caring that his face had hardened into a mask of stone.

"And you, Miss Flannery, are very quick to judge when you don't know all the facts. At any rate your mother has asked me to stay."

Her blue eyes blazed. "I wish I were a man! I'd throw you out of this house bodily."

His granite features softened slightly, and a mocking gleam of male challenge shone from his eyes as he let them roam casually over her. "Care to try it? I've always wondered what a wrestling match with you would be like."

Her Irish eyes snapped, but he ignored her wrathful gaze and went on silkily, "I don't have to guess how it would end up, though." His eyes dropped to her mouth.

"Think again, Mr. Deverone."

"You've already proven that you're still receptive to my kisses." He watched her, his mouth lazily forming the words. "I wonder what else you'd be receptive to—"

Like a female wildcat backed against the wall and fighting for her life, she faced him from her corner of the couch and bit out her answer. "Nothing that involved you, you can be sure of that." Her blue eyes glittered with pain. His physical presence was tearing her apart. She had to get him out of the house somehow. "Now, since we've solved that issue, will you please get dressed and leave?"

"Jamie is my legal son," he said slowly, as if he were measuring each word to test its effect on her. "I have a right to see that he's being properly taken care of."

He was questioning her ability to care for Jamie, hitting on the nerve that Judson had already probed that afternoon, and the double dose of male chauvinism sent her temper soaring to stratospheric heights. Her anger left her speechless for a second or two, and then she found her tongue. "You don't give a damn about the boy, and you know it."

"Don't I?" His brown eyes glittered with his own suppressed anger.

"You walked away from him, just as you walked away from Diane."

He leaned back, as if he were suddenly bored. "But now I'm back." The sound of a car bumping into the yard broke the silence that surrounded them and stopped the flow of her angry words.

"Are you expecting company?" Jord drawled. He was in control, coolly asking her the question, looking at her with a lazy assessment that made her feel as if she were a high-school girl being called for by a boy he disapproved of. Briefly she toyed with the idea of telling him it was none of his business and then thought better of it. "No." Oh, dear God, she was an emancipated woman—but she still didn't particularly care to have whoever it was find Jord in her living room dressed only in a robe. Gossip in a small town, once started, was difficult to halt. "I—I think your clothes must be dry by now. Why don't you go get dressed, and I'll see who it is."

For a moment she thought he was going to argue with her. But he didn't. When she turned her back on him to answer the door, she heard his quiet steps walking away from the living room, down to the basement.

The dusty orange Omni left little doubt about the identity of her caller. Judson Adams came around from the driver's side, his tall body moving easily in tan slacks and a silky white knit shirt. "Hello, Trisha. Marge seemed to think I should come and check up on you." He searched her face as if looking for signs of damage. Apparently satisfied that he saw none, his blond head swiveled as he surveyed the yard. "Is he still here? Where's his car?"

"His assistant dropped him off. Would—would you like to come in? We—we were just having coffee."

He gave her a slow smile. "I could use a cup." As they went through the porch to the kitchen Jud said from behind her, with that charm that was particularly his, "I have a bone to pick with you, you know. Since you didn't show up tonight, Marge drafted me to stand in for you." He leaned against the sink and watched her as she took down a cup from the cabinet and filled it with coffee.

"I'm sure it didn't hurt you to arrange a few plates and lay the silverware." She handed the cup to him, and he smiled a thank you, his eyes warm with regard.

"Only my male pride." He glanced down at the steaming liquid. "If I'm drinking from the same pot you brewed for Deverone, maybe I should ask you to taste this first."

She laughed softly, his pleasant banter a relief from the intense anger she had felt toward Jord. "I wouldn't let you drink anything fatal, Jud. Margie would come and scratch my eyes out."

Jud threw his head back and laughed. In this mood he was charming, the kind of man women always admired. Here in a small town, where everyone knew everyone else, there was little opportunity for extramarital affairs, and as far as Trisha knew, Jud had never indulged in a fling with another woman. But had he been so inclined, there would have been plenty of the opposite sex willing to sample his fair good looks and charm, she was sure. He had the knack of making a woman feel special.

They smiled at each other in quiet understanding, until his eyes flickered to a point beyond her shoulder. His smile faded, and a strange light flared in his eyes for a moment before they were shadowed by tawny lashes.

"Hello, Adams." From behind her Jord's voice sliced between them like a honed knife. He came into her line of vision, but he made no move to offer his hand to Judson. What right did he have to be so arrogantly rude to his cousin?

Judson nodded just as coolly. "Deverone." Judson's eyes flickered over the man's bare chest, the faded jeans. He said nothing about Jord's appearance. "What brings you to this part of the country?"

"Your wife invited me to a party," Jord said smoothly.

"I'm surprised you took time out of your busy schedule to come," Judson countered, an antagonistic edge in his voice.

"I thought it was time I checked on—my son."

Judson's eyes glittered, and there was an electric current of animosity between the two men that Trisha could almost feel. The fine hairs along her arm seemed to be standing on end.

"You're a little late, aren't you?" Judson dropped all pretense of friendliness. His words were cool and clipped:

"Maybe—and maybe not" was Jord's enigmatic answer.

Judson's lips tightened. He was visibly fighting to contain his anger. "I want you to know that if you've come to stir up trouble and try to take Jamie away from Trisha, you'll have me to contend with, Deverone."

Jord's eyes narrowed. He looked relaxed but dangerous, a man well used to confrontations with other men, a man who enjoyed pitting his strength against another. "What did you have in mind? A fistfight in the barn?"

Jord stood in the middle of the kitchen just to the side of Trisha with his feet planted solidly on the floor. Judson straightened away from the counter, put his coffee cup down, and faced Jord with fire in his eye. "That might do for a start." All his charm had vanished. Trisha was suddenly reminded of two battering rams, locked in combat.

"Stop it, you two," she ordered them sharply. "I won't have

you carrying on like ruffians in my house while Jamie is upstairs trying to sleep. Neither one of you is taking the boy away from me, and the sooner you understand that, the better off we'll all be."

The words, which were meant to relieve the tension between the two men, seemed to heighten it. Jord lost his lazy, taunting air. His body tightened, as if he had put every nerve on alert. "Adams wants the boy?"

"He's offered to adopt him," Trisha unwillingly admitted, "because of Margie."

"Because of Margie." There was a heavy weight of irony in Jord's voice that was inexplicable.

"Margie loves the boy," Judson said between gritted teeth. "And so do I."

"I don't doubt your love for him," Jord replied. "From what I've seen of him, he's an easy child to love. The question is"—his words became soft with intent—"what's best for him?"

"Jamie's ten times better off here than he would be living with you," Judson said tightly.

Jord's eyes narrowed, but he ignored the intended slur on his life-style. "For now, yes. But later—"

Judson's fists clenched at his sides. "Don't come here and remind us how wealthy you are, Deverone."

"I wasn't," Jord shot back. "I was merely saying that when it comes time to give the boy education beyond high school, I would be more than willing to finance his schooling—at any college he cares to attend."

"Like hell you will!" Judson's face was pale with anger.

"Hello! Is anybody home? Trisha? Jud? Where is everybody?" The lilting, feminine voice came from the general direction of the front door and was a welcome contrast to the hard tones of the men. Trisha would have welcomed any interruption at that moment, but she was especially grateful that her caller was her vivacious sister. Neither Jord nor Judson would be insensitive enough to continue their battle over Jamie in front of Margie

Adams. "We're in the kitchen," she called, her eyes fastened on Jord's face, their blue-violet brilliance alive with warning.

Margie, her petite body slim and attractive in white slacks and a sun-yellow blouse that contrasted well with her dark curls, appeared in the doorway. "What is this, a kitchen conversation? Hello, darling." She walked to Judson and kissed him lightly on the cheek. Trisha, watching, saw Jord Deverone's mouth tighten briefly.

"When you didn't come back," Margie mock-scolded her husband, "I begged a ride out here with Eleanor Jackson." She turned to Jord Deverone, her face glowing. "Jord. It's good to see you again." She held out her arms, and without hesitation Jord folded her into his. "Hello, Margie." He was so much taller, her head was buried in his chest. After a moment he held her away and smiled down into her face. "How have you been?"

After a heartbeat of hesitation she said, "Fine. But right now I'm exhausted. I've been on my feet all day, and they're starting to complain. Any chance I could talk you people into sitting down somewhere?"

"Go on in the living room," Trisha said. "I'll bring you some coffee."

"I could use some. Don't forget the splash of cream I like," Margie reminded her.

When they were settled in the other room, Margie and Judson on the couch together, Trisha and Jord in the chairs on each side, Margie sipped her coffee and then said, "Umm, I needed this. It's delicious, honey." She settled back in the couch. "Now, Jord, tell me. What are your plans? How long are you able to stay with us? You are staying with us, aren't you?"

Jord ignored the dark look on Judson Adam's face and shook his head. "I think I'll make my headquarters here for the next couple of days. Trisha needs some help mowing around the yard, and I've volunteered to give the buildings a fresh coat of paint while I'm here."

Trisha straightened in the wing chair and glared at him. "You'll do no such thing. I can manage on my own."

Jord shrugged one bare shoulder. "Why turn down the offer of free help?"

Trisha's eyes flashed, but Margie beamed at him. "It's wonderful of you to offer to help Trisha. And I'm glad you came early. Now you'll be here for the centennial."

"Centennial?"

"Arien is celebrating its one-hundredth birthday." Her smile widened, and just a touch of slyness tugged at her mouth. "We're having a beauty contest, you know."

"Now, that might be worth staying for," Jord drawled.

"I hoped you would think so," Margie said, grinning. "The contest is to decide who has the best-looking legs in Arien."

"That could be interesting," Jord agreed. "Who is entering the contest?" He glanced at Trisha, his eyes moving down the long shapely length of leg her denims did nothing to disguise even though she was seated.

"Oh, we're being very selective," Margie told him. "Only the best-looking men are allowed to enter."

"Men?" One of Jord's tawny eyebrows arched.

Margie laughed at him. "Yes, Jord. It's a contest to discover who has the best-looking set of male legs in Arien. Would you like to be considered as a contestant?"

"I'm not a native," Jord said easily.

"I know," Margie sighed. "I suppose that disqualifies you. I've been trying to get Jud to enter, but he absolutely refuses."

"It's nothing but a lot of nonsense you women have dreamed up," Judson said dismissively.

"But you have to admit it's created more interest in the centennial. We've had several calls from people in surrounding towns asking when the contest was being held, saying they didn't want to miss the event." She tilted her head and sent a laughing glance at Jord. "Grace Morrison, you remember her, Jord, her husband had a huge farming operation down by the lake before he died a few years ago, well, anyway, she is one of the judges, and she says she hasn't seen a man's bare leg in years, and she can't wait."

"Nothing but a lot of damn nonsense," Judson growled, repeating himself.

"You wouldn't say that if we were having women compete," Margie teased, laying her hand on his arm.

He looked down at her, his face softening. "I'm just glad you're not one of the judges," he said mock-warningly and brought his hand up to brush a fingertip down the length of her nose.

"That won't stop me from watching the contest," Margie retorted and smiled up at him.

"Well, just don't get any ideas," Judson said warmly. "I wouldn't want you running away with some other man and his dazzling legs."

"No chance," Margie breathed, looking up at him, her adoration shining from her hazel eyes.

Jord made a restless movement in his chair. "My suitcase is out in the pickup." He looked at Trisha, his eyes openly asking if she intended to refuse him accommodations for the night in the presence of Judson and Margie. "Do you have a flashlight? I'll have to walk out to the field and get it."

"Oh, don't do that," Margie said quickly. "Jud and I can drive you."

Jord shook his head. "No. I want a walk. I—need the exercise."

Trisha doubted that after the way he had worked that afternoon, but she said nothing. Jord, however, didn't move. Then she realized he was waiting, waiting for her to give her agreement to his request to stay here in the house, close to Jamie. And now that he had given her a choice, she lost the angry impetus to refuse him. He had, after all, made it possible for her to get the hay in and cover it before it was soaked beyond use. She did owe him something, if only a night's lodging. It wasn't that she was

68

afraid of him. He wouldn't force himself on her, she knew
If she stayed out of his arms and controlled her own feelin
would be perfectly safe. She had to do that. She couldn'
a replay of that scene in the barn. She lifted her head.
should be a flashlight in a drawer in the kitchen. I'll get it for
you."

It was an invitation to stay the night, and Jord knew it. "No,"
he said. "Don't get up. I'll find it." If there was triumph in his
eyes, he kept it carefully hidden from her and walked out of the
room.

"We should be going, Jud." Margie prodded him gently and
brought her small hand up to her mouth to stifle a yawn. "I'm
really tired."

"I'm ready any time you are," Judson told her and pushed his
long, lean frame out of the chair.

The windows of the porch threw squares of light on the lawn.
Judson was quiet as they went out through the dark night to the
car, Trisha walking behind them. But after he had opened the
door and settled Margie inside, he closed the car door and said
under his breath to Trisha, "Keep me posted."

She was startled for a moment, and then understanding
dawned. He wanted to be informed about any further moves
Jord might make to ingratiate himself with Jamie.

"I will," she promised softly.

She waved good-bye and watched the orange car make the
turn to go back down the lane. The clouds must have been blown
away by the storm; the black sky was brilliant with stars, stars
that sparkled like rare and precious gems that invited one to
reach up and grasp them. But if she were foolish enough to try,
those stars would burn and destroy her. They were incandescent,
magnetic, and dangerous—like Jord. His hands, his mouth set
fires blazing inside her. And he knew it. . . . The crickets were
playing their courting song, and from down in the barn, as if
Prince sensed her restless thoughts, the horse wickered low in his
throat. A breeze drifted across her cheek, scented with soft grass.

He wasn't there, but his presence seemed to fill her senses, [...]g him one with the night, making her want to return to [...]ht he had carried her cold and shivering body out of the water. . . . She stood staring out into the blackness and, at last, saw what her eyes had unconsciously been searching for, that beam of light that swung along on the ground.

No. This indulging in fantasies about a man she had known all her life had to stop. It was a subtle form of torture, a kind of sickness . . . she whirled around and went into the house. As she had always done, she concentrated on mundane tasks to take her mind away from emotional pain. She had things to do. She would have to make up the bed in the north bedroom with clean sheets and take the dust covers off the furniture. She was determined not to think beyond the moment, not to think of what it would be like trying to fall asleep, aware to the nucleus of every cell in her body that Jord Deverone lay in the next room.

Within a matter of minutes she had transformed Simon's bedroom from a cold, lonely place wrapped in dust covers to an inviting room ready for occupancy. She had folded the covers and tucked them away in the back of the closet, polished the heavy oak dresser and chest until they gleamed in the glow from the dresser lamps, and vacuumed the pale beige rug. Picking up the snowy white sheets she had retrieved from the linen closet, she shook them out over the double bed with a deft snap of her wrists. The fresh smell of linen dried in the open air drifted to her nose. A pool of light from the bedside lamp Simon had used for his nighttime reading illuminated a wrinkle on the surface of the top sheet. She smoothed it over the mattress and forced her mind away from the fact that Jord Deverone would come in here, undress, and lay his tall body down on the place she had prepared for him. She covered the sheet with a blanket he probably wouldn't need and struggled to block out the erotic images that floated to the surface of her mind . . . Jord undressing, his bronzed body emerging in the soft light . . . the sleek, tanned skin looking like dusky satin against the white linen . . .

She punched at the pillows in a helpless gesture of fury and raised her head to look around the room with an inspecting gaze. A slight breeze moved the cinnamon-colored drapes at the window, brushing the weighted corners against the shaggy threads of the light-beige carpeting. It wasn't the Ritz, but it would have to do.

"Is this where you want me?"

He stood in the doorway, watching her, his camel-colored carryall in his hand. Her heart leapt to a new, uncomfortable location. She had been so deep in thought she hadn't heard the pickup come into the yard or Jord's step on the stairs.

"Yes." Self-consciously she stepped away from the bed. "I'll get the suitcase caddy out of the closet—"

Before she had taken a step, he was inside the room, setting his case down and blocking her way. "You've already gone to enough trouble. Leave that to me. I can find it."

She stared at him, wishing she couldn't see the tanned sheen of his naked shoulders, the crisp body hair that invited her touch. Resolutely she pulled her eyes from him and missed seeing the dark flare of emotion in his.

She didn't tell him the thing he already knew, that there was only one bathroom on the second floor and they would have to share. "There are extra towels in the cupboard above the tub. Feel free to help yourself."

"I wonder what you'd do if I did," he said, reaching up and touching her cheekbone, making it clear that he wasn't talking about towels at all.

She flinched, feeling as if he had branded her with his warm fingers, hating him for rousing that quick, pulsing fire that raced through her bloodstream. "It wasn't meant literally."

"Pity." An undefined emotion flickered in his eyes. His hand dropped, and a cool reserve masked his features. He had withdrawn from her, and his rejection was more painful than she had ever dreamed it might be. "Good night, Trisha," he said huskily.

Her voice seemed to have deserted her. When she found it at

71

last, she said, "Good night, Jord," and knew she should be relieved that he had made no move toward her, but she felt strangely bereft as she walked past him and went out of the room. She was still awake when her mother came home.

The bright-yellow sun lit every corner of the kitchen. A summer breeze, cool and sensually pleasing, bathed her face as she stood at the sink and looked out over the farm. Everything was green and alive. The corn in the south field looked as if it had grown another foot during the night.

Sensing her lack of attention on him, Jamie squirmed on the curved bench of the breakfast nook and looked up at her from under long, silky lashes. His words tumbled out with a scarcely contained excitement. "Is he still here?"

She poured his orange juice and put it in front of him. Without thinking she smoothed her palm over the bright-gold cowlick and watched the hair spring upright the moment it was freed of the weight of her hand. "Yes, he's still here."

"Does he sleep late, or will he be up soon?"

Jamie's artless question and his calm assurance that she was acquainted with Jord's sleeping habits nearly choked her. She was saved from answering by a low, masculine voice.

"Good morning." Jord moved into the room. His wheat-colored hair shining clean, his jaw smooth and scented with expensive male cologne, dressed in well-worn denims and a T-shirt tautly stretched over his broad chest, he was no less devastating than he had been yesterday when she first saw him. Here, in her kitchen, the unfamiliar smell of well-groomed male mingled with the fragrance of dew-wet grass and rain-freshened air and did strange things to the muscles in her stomach. To make things worse, his eyes held a mocking gleam, telling her he had heard Jamie's question and knew full well why she hadn't answered.

"What would you like for breakfast?" she asked coolly, determined to keep the conversation and her thoughts on more prosaic things.

"Whatever the boy is having will be fine with me," Jord answered agreeably.

"He's having scrambled eggs and toast."

Jord nodded his approval. "That sounds good." His voice was still early-morning husky, and the thought occurred to her that she wasn't the first woman to hear those low, male tones at the beginning of the day and feel her senses stirred. The thought was not a pleasing one.

She finished scrambling the eggs, dished them out, and carried the plates to the table. Jamie made a sound of delight, and Jord added his soft, "Looks delicious."

She said thank you and settled down across from them. She should have been hungry after eating a light meal the night before, but the sight of Jord sitting beside Jamie did things to her throat and made eating a struggle that she eventually gave up. She settled for juice and coffee and was almost in control when Jord leaned back against the padded cushion and said, "That was very good. I can see why you're growing up so big and strong, Jamie. Does your Aunt Trisha feed you like that every day?"

"No," Jamie told him solemnly.

"No?" Jord raised an eyebrow and gave Trisha a quizzical glance.

"No," Jamie repeated. "Some days we have French toast, and on Sunday mornings sometimes we sleep late, and then we have waffles." He gave Jord a sober look. "Grandma's still in bed 'cause she was out so late last night."

"I see," Jord said. His tone was equally serious, but a smile tugged at the corner of his mouth.

"Do you like waffles?"

"Yes, very much."

"Then you should stay and sleep late with us on Sunday morning so you can have them," the boy said guilelessly.

Jord did smile then, no longer able to keep the gleam of amusement in his eyes hidden. Those brown eyes slid over Trisha's cool face. "Thank you for your kind invitation, Jamie. I'll—keep it in mind."

No longer able to stand his amused persual of her, she got to her feet. "If you'll excuse me, I have work to do."

Jord unfolded his long length from the curved seat and stood beside her. "What's on the agenda for today?"

The word was a blunt reminder of their divergent life-styles. "I don't have an 'agenda' for today, Mr. Deverone." Blue eyes flashed down the length of his lean body. "I merely have eighteen things to do, of which I'll only get four done."

"So what do you plan to start with?"

She turned away from him and began to collect the dishes. "My first priority is the west line fence. One of my steers broke off a rotted fence post and got into the neighbor's beans yesterday morning." *And I thought that was the worst thing that was going to happen.* "I dropped a temporary post in the existing hole, but it won't last. I've got to get out there and replace the post and tighten up the barbed wire."

She was picking up the toast plate when he took it from her hands. "Jamie and I can finish these. You go get your tools together, and we'll meet you outside in a few minutes. And I'd appreciate it if you could round up a pair of gloves I could wear. If I'm going to be handling barbed wire, I'll need a pair of gloves." His sardonic gaze moved over her, telling her that she was like barbed wire, prickly and sharp.

She stared at him for a moment, ignoring the double meaning in his words, wishing she could tell him to go away, wishing she could tell him she didn't need his help, but fixing fence was one of her least favorite jobs, and if he was fool enough to offer, she wasn't going to be fool enough to turn him down.

CHAPTER FOUR

The sun was already hot when they piled into the pickup and
jounced over the pasture to stop at the west line fence. Jamie
went to peer at the damage the cow had inflicted and shook his
head. "We're going to have to dig a new post hole."

"Is that your considered opinion?" Jord followed the boy over
to the fence and, after a quick look at the sagging fence post
leaning crazily in the too-big hole, nodded his head. "I think
you're right."

He was utterly unselfconscious as he stood at the back of the
pickup, stripped off his shirt, and pulled on the stained doe-
colored gloves that had been Simon's and that were almost too
tight for his long fingers, his sinewed hands. He grasped the
handles of the post-hole digger and pulled it across the open bed
of the truck. He handled its long length, its clumsily clanking
bucket-shaped cutters with the strength and ease of a fit man.
Bare shoulders gave off a tan sheen in the sun as he walked to
the offending post. A little to the right of it he started to dig, his
muscles rippling under his skin like the fine corded ribbing of
rope.

She watched, wishing there was some task she could do in

order to avoid seeing that full head of hair turn gold in the sun, that tall man's body moving with lithe ease as he brought down his weight on the edge of the shovel in rhythmic thrusts that bit into the black earth. The dirt was soft from last night's rain, and a rounded hole was rapidly appearing under the end of his booted foot, the mound of earth beside it growing.

She stood beside the cab, watching him, savoring the unaccustomed feeling of surrendering her work into capable hands. It had been a long time since she had felt that way. Simon hadn't been well, and she had, gradually over the last ten years, taken over many of his tasks. She could do everything there was to do on this farm, feed and load the cattle, plow, plant and harvest the crops, spray the corn, cultivate the beans, and later, walk through them, hoeing out the pesky cockleburs by hand. She had done it all last year with only an occasional helping hand from Judson. But now, having Jord share the work was a seductive thing, a bright idea that beckoned. She didn't have to be strong and independent always. Loren McAllister had been begging her to marry him for years. Maybe she should consider it. Maybe she did need a man . . . to be a father, a real father to Jamie. And Loren was fond of him. She wouldn't have been the first woman to marry a man who could care for a child. But her blood chilled at the thought of Loren taking her to his bed, making love to her. She had let him kiss her, but she had not let him make love to her. She wasn't prudish, she simply wasn't interested. She had sublimated that part of her life in her work on the farm. But sometimes, late at night, she lay in her bed, and thoughts of Jord would come trickling into her mind. It was as if he was in her bloodstream, lodged under her skin. At night, when a cool breeze blew across her body and touched her skin with the gentleness of a lover's hands, she thought of those moments in Jord's arms and turned into her pillow and wept silent tears. Those errant, sensual thoughts that attacked in the middle of the night had to be banished. She saw it more clearly than ever here, in the bright sunlight, watching his lithe body bend and twist.

His reality was not dangerous—it was her stupid little dreams, her adolescent longings that were dangerous. Jord had kissed her, yes. Once, long ago, and now again, yesterday, in the cool, shadowed darkness of the barn. Yesterday his kiss and his words made it clear that he wanted more than just kisses. But she was a country girl, worlds away from the sophisticated women he normally chose for playmates. Had he decided he needed a change of pace? The thought made her insides curdle. She grimaced, turning her head to watch Jamie.

He had discovered a toad, even though its brown body was so nearly the color of dried grass, and was pursuing it clumsily down along the fence line toward the maple tree that grew like a sheltering umbrella a few feet away, just on one side of the fence. He reached the tree, plopped down on the narrow border of grass under its shelter, and grinned back at her. Forcing her mind away from Jord, watching Jamie, she thought about her running battle with Clem Foster, her neighbor, on the subject of the maple tree. She'd had a discussion yesterday with him about it.

He had come over to complain about the steer getting into his beans. When she'd offered to pay for the damage, he had grudgingly admitted there hadn't been enough to warrant payment. Then, with characteristic contrariness, he'd switched to the subject of the tree. "Darn fool nonsense letting that tree stand just because it's old." His bright-blue eyes had glared at her. "Someday it will come crashing down on my head."

She had glared back at him, telling herself she didn't really wish his dire predictions would come true. "It's a solid tree, Clem, and there's no insect damage. I want it there as shade for my cattle." *And I want it there because it's been there since my great-grandfather homesteaded this place*, she could have added but didn't, since that would have made Clem even more livid.

"That should be deep enough," Jord said, tossing the posthole digger on the ground. He glanced up at her, and for a moment the look in his eyes startled her. They burned with some

77

undefined emotion. His face was cleanly illuminated in the sun, its hard, rugged male lines bathed with the faint sheen of perspiration. His forehead was beaded, and the tense line of his jaw was shiny. Was he overextending himself? That hardly seemed likely. His lean body had the fit look of a man who could run miles without tiring. The temperature was, however, climbing fast into the eighties and might hit ninety before the day was over.

His eyes flickered away, and he moved around to the back of the pickup. He reappeared, dragging the new fence post, and even in the open air she could smell the fumes of creosote, the resinate, oily preservative used to give the wood a reasonable life.

He lifted the post over the barbed wire and tamped it down, anchoring it in the soft dirt in the bottom. Using his foot and holding the post straight, he began to scrape the dirt back into the hole. She came to life then, grabbed up the shovel and moved to help him.

Conscious of the musky smell of him, she was careful to avoid touching him. They worked together at the task, hampered somewhat by the closeness of the post to the taut barbed wire. Carefully she averted her eyes from those powerful thighs, his bare shoulders.

When they had stamped the moist earth into an anchoring base for the pole, Jord turned to the task of freeing the wire from the wobbly post a foot away. Using pliers and a hammer, he braced himself with one gloved hand against the post and with the other pulled at the iron staples that held the three strands of barbed wire in place. The first one came out without too much difficulty, but the second one was stubborn.

"What did you do—weld this one in?"

"I wanted to make sure the same steer wouldn't nudge it loose. They never forget a weak spot in the fence once they've found it."

"Maybe you should consider electric fencing."

She shook her head. "Not as long as Jamie's around. Those darn steers can learn to stay inside the fence."

A smile tugged at his mouth. "And are you the one who's going to teach them?"

She didn't answer. He pulled the third staple loose easily and turned to squint out over the field. Against the green grass of the pasture the red backs of the Hereford cattle looked like rusty boats floating on a sea of green. A heat haze shimmered above the ground. One puffy white cloud floated in the north, a reminder of the rainstorm.

"How many head of cattle do you run, Trisha?"

"I have two hundred head right now. In the fall I'll be selling the feeders, and then I wait till spring to buy the new calves. That way I don't have so many cattle to feed hay to over the winter. I'm thinking of expanding the herd—if I get the courage to borrow even more money."

"Have you considered putting any of your land into set-aside acres?"

Her mouth tightened. "I can't afford to do that. Let the big farmers have the government pay them to let their land lay fallow."

"One of the main problems of the program is stubborn people like you who refuse to support it and continue to flood the market with your corn."

An irrational anger blazed inside her, made her put her hands on her hips and tilt her chin to look at him. She was uncomfortably aware that he was one of the few men in the world she had to tip her head to look up to. Her eyes snapped, her face rosy with more than the heat. "How do you know so much about bumper crops and set-aside acres?"

Casually, as if her anger were nothing that concerned him, he turned back to the post and pulled out the last staple. The wire snapped free. He tipped his head to met her fiery look with his own face cool and composed. "I read a lot."

"Well, don't let it go to your head." And with heated emphasis she added, "And don't try to tell me what to do."

He straightened and even in her anger she couldn't quite

79

understand how every movement he made could be permeated with that controlled power and authority that were so typically his. It was as if by merely standing on the land and touching it with the soles of his shoes, he made it his property . . . in the same way the touch of his hand on her body made her his. . . .

"I wouldn't think of telling you what to do, Trisha Flannery," he said softly, but the words sounded as if he had said, 'We'll duel at sunrise; chose your weapons,' there was so much challenge and mockery in them.

"You'd better not," she sputtered, horrified to hear the exaggerated consonants and the Irish lilt of her father's voice that came into her speech whenever she was disturbed. Fighting to hold her voice down and keep Jamie unaware of their confrontation, she said warningly, "You lost the right long ago to be involved in Jamie's life."

He straightened and gazed at her steadily. "But what about your life, Trisha? Have I lost the right to be involved in your life?"

She stared at him, her eyes locked in glittering combat with his. "My God! How can you even ask?"

"I can ask," he said softly, taking a step closer, "because I heard you tossing and turning in your bed last night. You didn't sleep very well, did you, knowing I was next door, knowing that a few short steps would bring you to my bed?"

"I lost him," Jamie announced from somewhere behind her. "I had him for awhile, but then he got away, and I couldn't find him."

She stood still, unable to tear her gaze away from those mesmerizing brown ones. Then with great difficulty she looked down at the blond head of his son. "Perhaps it's better for the toad, honey. After all, he likes to run around free, just like you do."

"I s'pose he does," Jamie agreed, his tone regretful, his eyes still squinting at the grass along the fence to see if he could spy another creature as interesting as his toad.

"We all like our freedom in one way or another," Jord said softly.

"Yes," Trisha said heatedly, thinking of Diane.

Jord shot her an angry look, and satisfied that she had scored a direct hit, she watched him turn back to the post. When the barbed wire was secure, he tossed the tools into the back. The three of them walked around to climb into the tattered front seat of the pickup. Trisha drove, and Jamie wriggled on the seat beside her. As she made the wide turn he said, "Can we go see the stone, please?"

Jord lifted a tawny eyebrow. "Stone?"

Trisha hesitated and then explained, "There's a cornerstone in the fence line. I—showed it to Jamie. It's the one James Flannery, his great-grandfather, put in after the Depression when he knew he wasn't going to lose his land like so many others had."

She hadn't wanted to share that bit of family history with Jord. But she had brought it on herself, she supposed, by telling Jamie about his great-grandparents. She had done it for a reason, to instill some pride in the blood he inherited from his mother. There would be those who would be only too eager to inform him about the circumstances of his birth. Let him at least find out about his mother's mistake of falling in love with the wrong man after he had gained an understanding of the toughness of the Flannery clan and their ability to cling to the land through the good times and bad.

She directed the pickup on its bumpy way toward the south corner of the field. When she stopped the vehicle, Jord opened the door, and Jamie bounded out.

The gray stone sat at a right angle to the line of fence, a square and stolid piece of concrete. But James Flannery's name cut in a crude inscription and the date, 1937, below were enough to make the stone special to Jamie. Two thirds of his name was spelled out in those jagged letters, and he stared at the stone with pleasure written on his face.

"Why is the edge chipped away like that?" Jord asked.

A faint smile played over Trisha's lips. "The story goes that the day it was poured, my grandmother decided she wanted to christen it. Grandfather James told her she'd better wait, that the concrete probably wasn't quite set yet. She told him he was crazy to worry about a stone, and what harm could a tap from a glass bottle possibly do?" Trisha smiled. "My grandparents were not drinkers and couldn't have afforded anything as extravagant as champagne anyway, so the only thing my grandmother had to break over the stone was a bottle of milk. She was a little too anxious. The concrete hadn't fully hardened, and my grandmother was not a small woman. She gave it a very ceremonial swing, my father said, and then watched in horror as the heavy glass of the milk bottle shattered and flew in all directions, taking with it a substantial corner of the stone. Grandpa was furious with her—wouldn't speak to her for days, my father said, not till he heard her on the phone pleading with the man who had poured the cornerstone to come out and do another. Grandpa James was so touched, they kissed and made up—and they never did get the stone fixed." Her mouth curved in recollection. "My father told the story very well."

"I'm sure he did." Jord's gaze was steady.

Oh, why was she sharing so much of herself, so much of Jamie? He didn't deserve it. She dropped her eyes and called to Jamie. "Come on, honey. I've got to get back to the house."

Even at a slow speed the pickup bounced over the pasture. Jord rested a bare arm on the window and seemed not to notice. Jamie was a welcome buffer between them.

The rest of the day went by in a blur of work. With Jord's help she got the bales of hay into the barn, using the sling and pulley, lifting several at a time after Jord had snugged the sling around them. By five o'clock the load was in the barn—even though the bales were stacked in a haphazard, dangerous way. But she insisted that Jord leave them. She didn't want to run the risk of having him suffer heat exhaustion in a one-hundred-and-ten-degree barn.

That night, after supper, her mother left for her women's church meeting, fretting about having to give devotions. "You'll do fine, Mother," Trisha assured her as she watched her climb into the neighbor woman's car.

A few minutes later she took Jamie out of the bathtub and put him to bed. With Jord safely downstairs watching television, she succombed to the urge to have a long, luxurious bath. The cool water felt like silk against her skin after the heat of the day. When she had finished, she swathed herself in her terry robe, toweled her black hair, and opened the door—and nearly collided with Jord.

"So you didn't fall asleep in the tub after all," he said, his eyes moving over her face bare of makeup, the silky tangle of hair.

"You weren't coming in to investigate, I hope," she said.

He continued to stand in her way, forcing her to lean back against the bathroom door, making it impossible for her to pass. He wore a cotton denim shirt in a standard blue color with the cuffs rolled back and denim pants, but no man had ever looked more devastating in simple work clothes. Her throat constricted, making normal breathing impossible.

"As a matter of fact—I was." He said it deliberately, waiting for her reaction.

"I would have made you sorry if you had," she said with a forced lightness of tone and stared up into his face, her eyes sparkling with little blue flames.

"I imagine you would have—tried," he murmured. "And I would have enjoyed the—trying." He reached out to smooth a tendril of dark hair off her terry-clad shoulder.

"Don't—" The word was an outcry, far too revealing. She struggled for control. "—touch me." The last two words were low, but there was an undertone of savagery in them, her whole body singing with the tension of a tightly strung wire.

"Has anyone ever told you how primitive you are, Trisha Flannery?" he said slowly, as if she hadn't spoken at all. "How your pupils flare because the emotion you try to repress is so

83

strong? You're like a wild colt that alternately dances close to danger and then shies away."

"You flatter yourself," she said fiercely.

"No." Jord's face was devoid of emotion. "You want me to kiss you—just as much as I want to taste that warm mouth again—" He pulled her into his arms, and even through the terrycloth she could feel the rough determination of his hands, the hard muscles of his thighs, the sharp imprint of his belt buckle against her stomach. His head lowered to hers, moving closer, and there was nothing she could do, nowhere to run. She twisted her head to the side in a desperate attempt to avoid his mouth.

He laughed softly, and then she felt his tongue flick against the ear she had made vulnerable to him. Its moist warmth explored the shell of her ear, the lobe, the tiny hollow scented from her bath. Desire began its low, sweet hotness inside her, and she was fast losing the will to resist. She twisted her head to escape his marauding tongue. "Jord, please—"

His mouth closed over hers, and all other sensations were forgotten as he claimed her with the same primitive savagery he had accused her of having. He was male possessing female, wooing and seducing with mouth and tongue and hands. His grip moved lower, cupping the curves of her hipbones, holding her against him, making no secret of his desire for her.

A wild recklessness surged through her blood and swept away the last remaining barrier. She molded herself against him and opened her mouth to his caresses, returning the sensual exploration of his tongue with light little caressing flicks of her own.

"Trisha." Her name came into her mouth on his shuddering breath. He scooped her off her feet and into his arms, and at once the old self-consciousness swept over her. She was a tall girl, and no man had ever picked her up and carried her. "Put me down, Jord."

He silenced her protest with a kiss, and then she was being lowered gently to the flower-sprigged spread of her bed. He followed her down, his mouth seeking and finding the warm pulse at the base of her throat exposed by the wrap neckline of her robe. Then his fingers moved to the tie. She wanted to stop him, she knew she should stop him. But the house was silent, the night dark and close around them, and a soft summer breeze feathered over her face and along the backs of her hands. His mouth at her throat seemed to be connected with the source of her life. She needed more, needed to feel those lips touching all of her. She made a restless movement, pushing her chin up, which only exposed the curve of her neck further, and his mouth traveled upward and nibbled along the way. He coaxed and seduced and persuaded, and she melted under the heat of that mouth touching her cheeks, her eyelids, her temples. Her dream of him and reality merged, making her body shiver with sweet longing.

He pulled the tie free and pushed back the edges of her robe with a light brush of his fingers. In the faint moonlight streaming in the window her body gleamed like pearl satin. He breathed in harshly. "You're not real," he said hoarsely. "You can't be—"

He couldn't be real either, even though she could smell the clean masculine smell of him and feel the rough fabric of his shirt under her fingers. He was a dream, a dream she must grasp and hold before she woke. She lifted her arms and clasped them around his neck, aching for the pressure of his mouth on hers.

For what seemed like an endless moment he delayed the downward movement of his head. His eyes gazed into hers, as if he, too, were caught in a trance. Then his resistance melted, and he breathed in sharply and let her pull his head downward. "Dear God," he murmured. "This can't be happening." His mouth opened, moved against hers, tenderly, possessively. His tongue found hers, teasing, enticing. She answered his tantalizing caresses with her own, her tongue thrusting against his until he groaned, a soft, tortured sound. Still kissing her, he traced the hollow of her throat with reverent fingertips, and then trailed his hand down a slow, sensuous journey over her flesh to the valley of her breasts. He circled the soft mounds teasingly, coming close to the taut peaks, which quivered, but not quite touching them. His fingertips found new places to explore, the sensitive underside of her breast, the hollow of her shoulder, the crest of her collarbone, yet never came close to the rosy buds which ached for his touch.

She made a distressed little sound in the back of her throat, and he raised his head and looked down at her. "What is it?"

"Jord, please—"

"Is something wrong?" His voice held the satisfied amusement of a purring tiger.

Aching with torment, determined to give him just a small sample of the torture he was inflicting on her, she reached for him, finding the smooth buttons of his shirt in the dark, unfastening them, increasingly aware that his teasing fingers were still working their ravishing magic on her throat, shoulders, and arms, brushing lightly over every inch of her upper body but the most sensitive part until she had to bite her lips with the effort not to cry out. Her only defense was an offense, and she tugged at his shirt, pulling it half out of his belt. Instinct directed her, and unlike him, she placed her hands directly over his male nipples. She brushed lightly over the hard male buds and felt their immediate response to her touch.

"You little witch," he muttered with a low intensity that thrilled her. He moved suddenly, and with controlled passion his fingers gave her the satisfaction she craved. His hand brushed her taut peak, circled and then claimed it with a possession that fanned the flames of her desire.

She sighed with satisfaction, but he had only begun the sensual onslaught. Now his mouth took the place of his hand at her breast, and his tongue lavished erotic attention on her. Fire bursts of desire seemed to explode in her lower body. She moved restlessly, and he shifted, trailing his mouth across her heated skin, finding her other breast and slowly building the fires within her all over again. She slid her hands under his loose shirt and raked her nails gently down the length of his spine, feeling his answering shudder with an intense, possessive pleasure. He kissed the palm of her hand and expertly eased one arm out of her robe. She leaned forward to make his task easier, and he favored her with a burning kiss on the tip of her shoulder. Her other arm was freed of the restraint. His mouth sought her breast again while his fingers wandered lower, over the flatness of her stomach to her navel. He explored its small circle and then tantalizingly moved lower still, to the sweet femininity of her. His hands and mouth were pleasing her, teasing her, and totally destroying her. The onslaught on her senses made her gasp out the cry that had been hovering on her lips.

The sound echoed through the quiet house—and in a subconscious response Jamie cried out, his voice high and piercing and caught on the edge of a dream.

She roused up at once, and desire slid away. "I must go to him."

"No, stay here," Jord ordered. "He's quiet now."

"He may be awake and frightened. Let me go."

With a short, muttered curse Jord released her and pulled away.

She stood up, wrapped her robe around her fevered body, and tightened the tie at her waist, conscious of Jord watching her from his half-sprawled position on the bed behind her. She turned her back to him and walked out the door, her mind in a tangled confusion of thought.

The hall was dark, but she found her way by long habit and turned the corner into Jamie's bedroom. He was, as Jord had guessed, already asleep again. He slept with his chin tucked into his chest, the sheet kicked off, the jacket of his yellow pajamas twisted around his little-boy body. His feet looked bare and very—Jamie. He was her sister's son—and Jord's.

A cold chill, a shiver of jealousy, clogged her throat, clenched her teeth. She was jealous of her sister, jealous of the love she had shared with Jord. But nothing could change her feelings toward the boy who lay there sleeping, looking so young and vulnerable. She tucked the covers around his feet and went out of the room.

As if he had known exactly how she would feel when she came back into the room, Jord was standing by the window, well away from the bed, his back to her, his profile in the dark room tall and male.

She flipped on the light switch, and he turned. His shirt hung open, the shirt she had unbuttoned with eager fingers. "Is he all right?"

"Just a dream." She tried to avoid looking at him and only succeeded in bringing the mussed covers on her bed into her vision. She twisted her hands and fought for coolness. "Jord, I think you'd better go."

"Out of your room—or out of your life?"

The question was quiet, lacking any tone of mockery. If he was surprised at her request, he didn't show it. Not a muscle in his face moved.

And somehow his stoic acceptance made her waver in her determination. "For tonight—out of my room."

"And tomorrow?" A light eyebrow angled upward.

"Tomorrow I—think—you should go—out of my life."

"Why?" he asked reasonably. "Because you're letting me get too close? Because tonight I nearly succeeded in making you admit what you've been denying for years?"

"There's nothing to admit or deny, Jord," she said in what she hoped was a cold tone. "I was—caught up in the heat of the moment." Her mouth twisted. "After all, you are a practiced lover."

He didn't rise to her jibe. "And that bothers you?"

"You made love to my sister."

"No," he said softly, "never." He took a step closer. "Think about it, Trisha. If I had, why would I bother to lie to you about it? Why do you think I've let you keep Jamie all these years? Don't you think I would have come and claimed the boy if he were really mine?"

"You don't want him—"

"He isn't mine to have," he repeated softly, and his brown eyes glittered with something that disturbed and confused her.

"Stop it!" she cried. "I won't listen to your lies—"

In two steps he was beside her, pulling her into his arms. "Right now I don't give a damn whether you believe me or not. All I know is that no other woman makes me feel the way you do when I hold her in my arms . . . and I'd be willing to bet that no other man makes your heart race like it's racing now. . . ."

His hand moved under the folds of her robe, finding the soft curve that pulsed with the rapid heartbeat he had known he would find.

"No, damn you, leave me alone—"

He smothered her protest with his hard, insistent mouth, kissing her with a fierce passion that bent her to his will. Then, even as she began to struggle angrily, the kiss ended, and she was free.

"Now," he said huskily, "I'll leave you to your precious sense of honor—and your solitary bed."

With a slight mocking bow of his pale gold head he left her. She stood frozen as he brushed past her, unable to breathe, unable to think.

But a few minutes later, when the light in his room had clicked out and she heard his weight settle on the mattress of her stepfather's bed, she had plenty of time to breathe—and to think.

None of her thoughts were comforting. No amount of rationalization could change the fact that Jord was right, that she had almost given herself to him—thinking of nothing but the heaven he had allowed her to glimpse in his arms. Oh, God, how could she live with herself after this night? And yet, that niggling thought, that one nugget of truth kept repeating in her brain: *I would have come and claimed the boy if he were really mine—*

For the first time ever she considered the problem of Jamie from Jord's viewpoint. True, Jamie would have hindered his jet-setting life-style. But Jord was a wealthy man. Even if he didn't want to personally involve himself in Jamie's life, he could well afford to send the boy to private school or hire a woman to care for him. And something told Trisha that's exactly what he would have done if Jamie were his son. It was not logical that an arrogant man like Jord Deverone would allow his son to grow up nearly two thousand miles away from him, almost totally ignorant of his father's existence. But if Jord was not Jamie's father—who was?

No, the whole idea of Diane with another man was impossible. Diane had repeatedly told Trisha how much she loved Jord and how he had simply left her when her pregnancy had made her big and cumbersome and too needful of sleep to keep up with the schedule of nighttime activities he loved. And each time Diane retold the story, it was like a knife sliced through Trisha's heart.

Against the clean sheets, in the brief cotton gown her skin burned. How could she still want him? But she did. She ached with wanting the fulfillment her body had been denied, while her brain went around in endless circles, asking questions. She made a slight movement—and heard an answering rustle of bedclothes from the room next door. Damn him! He was lying awake, listening, knowing that she was in agony, denying with her mind what her body was aching to have. . . .

In the cool dawn she awoke to a quiet house. Her head ached, and the spiral of thoughts that had kept her awake the night before started all over again. But this time she didn't have to lie there. She could get up, get out of the house. She used the bathroom and dressed in a snug yellow T-shirt and denim pants. To get to the stairs, she had to pass by Jord's door. It was open. Of their own will her eyes lifted. She saw him then, lying on his side facing her, long gold lashes against darkly tanned cheeks, a light covering of springy golden hair on his bare torso, the top sheet wrapped around his lower body. The clear outline of hip and thigh and leg made it evident that he was sleeping in the nude. She knew she shouldn't have been looking at him, but she

90

couldn't turn away. Her eyes seemed to be riveted to the well-shaped face, the molded jaw, the hair like gold that even in sleep looked full and alive around his head.

He made a restless movement, his hand clenching and unclenching. Her face on fire, she whirled and noiselessly walked down the hall.

Jamie, too, was still sleeping. He lay in the same position as Jord, his body turned to one side, his arm lying along his body. Lashes the exact shade of Jord's fanned against his cheek. He was Jord's son—he had to be.

Color drained away from her face. Foolish hope died. Her hands caught at the doorframe, groping for something, anything, to help her withstand the blow. Her head reeling, her eyes blurred with tears, she stumbled down the stairs and out of the house.

She brushed away the tears and held her head high as she walked across the yard. Her fingers were clumsy on the hook and eye of the barn door.

"Hello, Prince." The horse danced sideways in anticipation of freedom. He moved restlessly while she saddled him, eager shivers running along his flanks.

Afraid of waking Jord, she held the horse to a quiet walk in the yard, but when they were halfway down the lane, she gave him his head, and he lengthened his stride till his mane streamed over her fingers in a river of black silk. Every movement of his body eased the tension from hers. At the end of the lane she turned him north, and they flew down the gravel road toward Silver Lake. This morning, in the pale yellow light, it almost lived up to its name. The silvery surface was smooth as a mirror, unbroken by even the smallest ripple. The willows and cottonwoods surrounding the shoreline were like mannikins, their curved reflections a still-life painting.

The tears and indecision blew away, as she knew they would. There was no choice for her, really, and there had never been. Jord would go, and life would revert to its calm stillness, a stillness like that of the lake. There would be no magic, no wild excitement wrought from the mere touch of a fingertip . . .

She let Prince turn down into the old lake road, the one close to the shore. The weedy path was overgrown. It was not a popular spot. People drove fifteen miles north to Lost Island for swimming, and farther still to the big twin lakes of Okoboji for boating and fishing. But in other years the lake had been used for recreation. She had come here to swim with the gang, Diane, Jord, Judson, and Margie years ago. She supposed it wasn't that long, really. But now those carefree summer days seemed like events that had happened to another person. It was on one of those hot nights that she had gone out into the water too far and known she was going to drown until she found Jord at her side. He had growled softly, "You little fool," and carried her ashore. . . . She cursed softly. She had come riding to forget Jord, not indulge in an orgy of remembrance and regret. She turned for home.

In the shadows of the barn something moved. She gasped.

"Don't panic," Jord ordered, stepping into the light. "It's only me."

"I didn't expect to see you here, that's all." Her voice was crisp, a reaction to the emotions that were clamoring at her stomach. She remembered the last time they had stood together in the barn . . .

"I want to talk to you."

She tethered Prince and bent over to unbuckle the cinch belt. "I think we said all we have to say to each other last night."

"Not quite." He hesitated and then stepped forward and took the saddle from her. The shoulder and arm muscles rippled under his pale cream cotton shirt as he swung it to the rack behind him. The shirt was teamed with denim pants and western boots, a casual outfit that was definitely not his traveling clothes. Her nerves tightened.

"I thought we agreed you'd be going this morning." Purposely she turned away from him and began to rub down Prince's gleaming ebony flanks with a soft cloth.

"Did we? I don't remember that." He was cool and contained, not the least disconcerted by her words.

She stroked the horse's flank and then moved to the other side of him. "You have a poor memory—for a lot of things, Mr. Deverone," she said coolly.

"Strange you should say that. I think you are the one who has a poor memory."

She tossed the cloth she had been using aside and recklessly courted danger. "What would you like me to remember?"

He stared at her, a slow, mocking smile on his mouth. "That Margie believes I'm here to do some painting."

It was a quick verbal sidestep that she hadn't anticipated. "Painting?"

"The barn needs a coat of paint. So does the machine shed. I can rent a sprayer and get the job done in the next two days."

He had to know he was hitting her in a vulnerable spot. She had been unhappy about the way the buildings looked, their red faded to a dull rust color, but she hadn't had the time or the money to do anything about it. She still didn't, but she said coolly, "All right. I'll pay you."

She expected him to protest, but he didn't. "What would you say I'm worth—an hour?"

There was a mocking note, a sexual innuendo that brought a wicked gleam to her eyes. One well-shaped eyebrow flew up, and her mouth curved in a smile. "Conservative estimate?"

An answering glitter of amusement burned in his. "No. Be extravagant."

A number of tart replies hovered on her lips. But the one that came out was cool and provocative, and it kept the sexual innuendo alive. "I haven't had much experience in—hiring men. But isn't it true that when you pay by the hour the worker tends to—stretch the job out to raise the price?"

His mouth quirked. "Is that what you think I'd do?"

"You might." She knew she shouldn't be bantering with him this way, but the subtle sexual tension that flowed between them made her feel wildly alive, the way she might have felt walking a tightrope over an abyss.

"Then perhaps I'd better get paid a lump sum."

"Perhaps you'd better," she mocked.

"I'll take the pickup to Emmetsburg and get the paint and the sprayer."

She saw it then, the neatly planned move that had maneuvered her into doing exactly what he wanted her to do. She dropped the cool, bantering manner and struck at him with words, probing at the place where she knew he was most vulnerable. "Let's stop playing charades, Jord. Your time is money, I would think. You can't afford to spend it on menial labor."

He stared at her, a dark flame lighting those brown eyes. "Perhaps I can't afford not to."

It was an ambiguous statement that could have meant anything—or nothing.

"Therapy?" she mocked.

He seemed to relax and said in a slow drawl, "Call it an attempt to get away from it all."

She let a shoulder lift and fall. "I'd hate to think I stood between you and your peace of mind."

"You've always done that," he said softly, "from the first moment I touched you." He moved closer, as if to reach for her.

"Stop it," she ordered him sharply, flattening herself against the cool concrete wall, a shiver of revulsion chilling her.

The dark stain of anger colored his cheeks. His hands dropped to his sides. "You've decided to play it safe, have you?" There was a hard, cold edge in his voice that she had never heard before. "But where does that leave me? Am I supposed to go back to the city and forget that for a few moments I held a warm and responsive woman in my arms last night?"

Her knees trembled. The words clogged in her throat, but she forced them out. "You must."

It cost her the earth to meet that cool, derisive stare with her head thrown back, her eyes challenging, but she did it. Then his face changed, hardened with decision. "All right. We'll play it your way. If you'll agree to let me stay here with—Jamie, I promise it will be on your terms. I won't touch you—" He paused and then said softly, "unless you ask me to."

"That will be a cold day in July," she grated.

Her vehemence seemed to restore his amusement. "The weather in Iowa is unpredictable in any season. Tornados, rain, hail, snow, and sometimes on the same day. Who knows what might happen?"

"The sun is shining, Mr. Deverone, and the weather report states that the temperature will peak out in the low nineties for the rest of this week with no relief in sight. Does that answer your question?"

"The weather, like the human race, is highly unpredictable, Miss Flannery."

"Some people," she said, "are very predictable."

He shrugged and turned away, his hand going to the door.

"I can only afford to pay you two hundred dollars," she said crisply to his back.

He opened the door and stepped through, turning back to hold it for her. There was a dark, unreadable look on his face. "I accept."

She walked from the barn into the sunshine, feeling unaccountably disturbed. Surely she had the best of the bargain. She had hired him to paint her buildings at a ridiculously low fee, and he had promised to stay away from her. Then why did she feel so uneasy—as if she had made a stupid move on a chessboard that would later cost her the game?

They ate breakfast as they had the morning before, Jord sitting beside Jamie, eating the food she had cooked. When they finished, Jamie pleaded to be allowed to ride with Jord into town. Trisha gave her reluctant permission and later went to the window to watch Jord help the boy into the cab. He lifted the boy up, his large hand fitting easily over Jamie's small bottom. Trisha turned away, her heart beating in an agitated rhythm she couldn't control.

Two hours later they returned, and Jamie came into the kitchen clutching a small gray kitten.

"The man at the store had them in a basket and said there were too many. Jord said I could keep it if you said so. Please, Aunt Trisha, can I keep him?"

She sighed and raised her eyes to Jord. The brown eyes were cool. "I told him it would be his responsibility to see that the animal was fed and watered. He is old enough to understand that a pet has to be cared for. He also understands that if you say no, the kitten goes back."

"Please, Aunt Trisha?" Imploring brown eyes lifted to hers. "I'll take real good care of Misty, honest."

"You've already given it a name—"

"I had to. I couldn't just call it *her* all the way home."

She had never been able to look into those beautiful brown eyes of her nephew's and refuse him something he wanted that was within reason.

"If you promise to take good care of her and feed and water her at mealtimes, I have no objection."

"Oh, thanks. Umm, I love you," he said to Trisha, holding the kitten cradled in one arm and wrapping the other around her. The kitten meowed a protest.

Instantly Jamie pulled away from Trisha and held the kitten up to scan her with worried eyes. "I'm sorry, Misty. I didn't mean to hurt you." Anxiously he looked up at Trisha. "Can I give her some milk? The man said she could drink it from a saucer."

"Yes, of course. I'll get you some."

She raised her head and caught a glimpse of a strange look in Jord's eyes, a look of pain. Before she could fathom what that look meant, the kitten jumped down out of Jamie's arms and scampered toward the back porch. It took the saucer of milk

Trisha poured to coax the kitten within Jamie's reach, but once the animal smelled the milk, she was docile enough. Trisha left the two of them on the floor of the porch, the cat's pink tongue lapping the milk into its mouth, Jamie crooning and running stubby fingers over the gray back.

Jord's face had returned to its normal lean, sardonic lines. "I hope I haven't complicated your life."

You've done that since the first summer you came here. She shook her head and managed to say, "No. It's probably a good thing to have a cat around for a change. She'll be no trouble."

Even in the short time he was gone with Jamie, the house had seemed empty. Now that he was back, he seemed to fill the room, make it too small. She turned away to grip the edge of the sink and stare out the window.

Jord said, "Well, I suppose I'd better get to work."

Unwillingly she turned back to look at him. "You should change your shirt. Do you have an old one?"

His slow smile nearly undid her. "I'll find something."

CHAPTER FIVE

Margie drove over early that morning and asked her mother to come and help pick and freeze the peas that were ripening in the garden. Mrs. Adams went, leaving Trisha alone to fight the temptation to watch Jord as he painted. All that day she found herself turning like a magnet to look at him. He stood at the peak of the barn on the scaffolding he had built, his blue-clad body outlined against the red siding. She stared at him, warring emotions chasing through her, shame because she had allowed him to begin painting when she wasn't sure if he could stand the physical stress, anger because he deserved it. He had volunteered for the job, she hadn't asked him, and it was a job that she desperately needed done. Why was it that Jord managed to fill her with conflicting emotions no matter what he did?

She carried feed to Prince, thinking that at least when she was in the barn, she couldn't crane her neck to look up at Jord. But toward the middle of the morning she had to return to the house, and her eyes swung back to the blue figure outlined against the red building, and it was then she saw that the heat had begun to affect him. He had changed into a blue long-sleeved denim shirt to protect his arms from the paint spatters, and the dazzling heat had brought out a dark round blot of perspiration on his back. The sight of his soaked shirt gave her a galling attack of conscience. She shouldn't have allowed him to do this. But he already had the peak and a substantial part of the top half done. The contrast between the weathered portion and the freshly painted wood was dramatic.

She expected him to stop for lunch, but he didn't. She paced the floor in the kitchen, watched the minutes click by on the big clock above the cabinet, and at one o'clock she could stand it no longer. She went out of the house and walked the length of the yard. From beneath the ladder she said, "Come down and have something cold to drink and a sandwich." Her voice was brusque, commanding.

"In a minute—"

She gripped the ladder and tried to control her temper. "No, now. I won't have you collapsing of heat exhaustion."

He looked down at her. "Is that a direct order from my employer?"

She wasn't amused. She was, in a way, responsible for him, and if anything happened, they were a long way from medical help. That was one of the disadvantages of living in the country. "Yes," she said shortly, "if that's the only way I can get you down here."

Jamie sat watching from under the shade of a tree that was close to the barn. His legs were bent, Misty cradled in his lap. He had been warned by Jord to stay away from the ladder and keep a firm hold on the kitten.

They elected to eat lunch out on the picnic table under the shade of a cottonwood. Jord washed his face and hands in the pan of water that Trisha provided and dried himself on the dark-green towel. Jamie watched, his eyes wide.

Trisha stifled a resentment that was growing with every minute of Jamie's wide-eyed attention and said to Jord, "Would you like ham and cheese or something different?"

"Whatever you're having is fine." Under his breath to her he murmured, "If we're having salad, I hope the lettuce is as crisp as you are."

"What I am is none of your business," she muttered, setting out the chips and the pitcher of lemonade.

She sat down on the picnic bench and distributed the sandwiches on paper plates, her mouth firm. Jord was across from her, his back to the distant barn. Jamie, with a shy, almost adoring look, eased down next to him.

A light, capricious breeze sprang up and made the leaves of the cottonwood rustle. The breeze lifted a strand of Jord's pale gold hair. Her irritation at Jord's remark melted away, and she let the marvelous sensation she couldn't identify sweep over her. What was it? It was something she had not felt in a long time. Was it contentment? It was more than contentment, really. It was a deep sense of belonging, of being one with everything around her, the blue sky, the panorama of fields and cattle, of satisfaction at having Jamie munching on his sandwich on the seat across from her. Jamie? Was it Jamie's presence that gave her this sense of euphoria? She dropped her eyes to the table and saw the ordinary things that had been there when she had provided lunch for Simon and Jamie: paper cups, paper plates, those last few crumbs of potato chips which Jamie never ate and which would soon be scattered to the birds. She stared at the red-checkered cloth—and knew that it wasn't Jamie's presence that made her feel lighthearted. It was Jord, casually resting his elbows on the table now that he was finished with his sandwich, who made her feel complete. It was the strength of those muscled arms exposed by the rolled sleeves of his shirt, the sight of his hair blowing attractively around his head, the hard line of jaw and throat that somehow gave her life meaning. Dear God, that was impossible. Jord didn't belong here. And he didn't belong to her.

"Would you like some more lemonade?" she asked huskily.

As if he had caught the emotional tone in her voice, he glanced up at her, his eyes narrowed in a questioning look. "Yes."

Jamie bounced on the seat beside Jord and said, "Can I go get Misty now?" He had followed Trisha's orders and deposited the kitten in the back porch while they ate. She had warned him to keep careful watch on the little cat until the animal became familiar with the farm.

"Clean up your place, and then you may go," she told him calmly.

Jamie flew away, his small feet churning over the grass.

"If I clean up my place, may I go?" Jord's voice dryly mocked her.

"I'll take care of everything," she answered crisply, taking his question at face value, refusing to rise to the bait. She stood up and began to clear, stuffing the debris into the paper bag she had brought for that purpose. "Simon used to stretch out on the grass and take a nap after lunch. I suggest you do the same. Or don't you allow yourself to snatch a nap occasionally?"

She looked at him then, her blue eyes cool with challenge, her hair lifting about her head as the breeze freshened.

Unhurriedly he let his eyes wander over her unmade-up face, her tangled hair. "If I didn't, I'd be a very tired man most of the time."

"I have some bookwork to do, and I'll keep Jamie and his furry friend out of your hair for the next half hour," she offered.

"That's an offer I can't resist," he murmured.

The thought of seeing him stretched out on the grass gave an added urgency to her desire to clear the table quickly. She stuffed everything into the bag, grasped it in one hand, and picked up the lemonade pitcher with the other. She pivoted to go, but his voice stopped her, made her turn back.

"Thanks for the lunch," he drawled, "and the suggestion that I rest. Nice to work for such a considerate employer."

She stood at the end of the table clutching the bag and the pitcher in front of her and met his mocking gaze steadily. "I'm glad you appreciate your good fortune." Not wanting him to think she was concerned about him, she added unthinkingly, "The pay is so low I have to extend a few fringe benefits."

He lifted a pale gold eyebrow. "Oh?" He gazed leisurely down the length of tanned leg that was visible beneath the frayed denim cutoffs she wore. As if he were saying it aloud, his eyes reminded her that last night he had seen much more of her. "Yes. I seem to remember—one or two."

His evident enjoyment in remembering made her skin burn. "Jord, about last night—"

"What about last night?" he asked, his voice smooth, his eyes watchful.

"It—can't happen again."

He seemed to relax. "At least you're not stupid enough to say it meant nothing to you."

"Of course it meant something to me. I don't normally allow any man to—"

"Get that close to you?" He captured her eyes with his.

"No." It was a fierce, husky denial. "I've—been made love to before, but—"

His face hardened, and then he shrugged as if he had lost interest in the conversation. "You're infringing on my nap time."

His cool lack of interest in discussing their personal relationship hurt. He simply wasn't interested in her thoughts or feelings. He had merely been caught up in the heat of the moment. "I'm sorry," she said. "I won't mention it again."

He murmured something, but she didn't hear it. She turned her back to march away over the grass toward the house, her mind churning with anger and embarrassment.

When she finished cleaning up the kitchen, her frame of mind was much the same. She felt disturbed and confused. Her state of mind worsened when, after she had gone into her small den, gotten out the books, and settled down to do the hated paperwork, she heard the phone ringing in the kitchen. Her irritation faded when she recognized the caller's voice. It was Margie. "Mom and I are going great guns. We already have ten quarts in the freezer." Then with a breathless change of subject that was typically Margie, she asked, "Has Loren said anything to you about the dance tomorrow night?"

"No." A feeling of dismay nagged at her. She really didn't want to go to the dance at all. And she didn't want to see Loren.

"Well, if he doesn't, Judson and I will be over around seven to pick you up. And Jord, too, if he wants to go."

"I'll—ask him."

Margie chatted on about the decorations and arrangements for the dance, and Trisha listened, though her thoughts were not on her sister's words. It was a relief when Margie finally said she'd better get back out to the garden and help her mother.

Margie brought her mother home around six o'clock, and by then Jord had finished painting the north side of the barn. He came in, and Trisha seated them at the table. She had prepared a tasty meal of chicken and potato salad and cole slaw, and her mother expressed appreciation of the food.

"My, it's nice to eat someone else's cooking."

Jord, after flicking a glance at Jamie, who was absorbed in biting into a chicken leg, made a satisfied sound and sat back. "You taught your daughter well, Ginny."

"Why, thank you, Jord. You always were so appreciative of my cooking."

Appreciative? Trisha couldn't remember that. He had seemed to her to be a mocking, self-contained male even in his early twenties.

"I appreciated all the things you did for me," Jord said softly. "I'm sure it wasn't the easiest thing in the world, having your husband's nephew pawned off on you each summer." Jord smiled at Mrs. Adams, a smile full of charm. "After all, you already had Judson, your new stepson, to take care of, as well as your own girls."

Ginny Adams smiled. She was in her late fifties, but her face was smooth, her complexion clear. Only the beginning of a wrinkle lurked on her forehead. "I considered myself lucky. I had always wanted a son—and each summer I had two of them."

"I was lucky you thought of me that way."

"I still do," Mrs. Adams said, giving him a clear-eyed look, and for a moment there was a heavy little silence, as if some form of communication was going on that Trisha didn't understand. Then, as if to lighten the mood, Mrs. Adams laughed shortly and said, "I've always had a soft spot in my heart"—this without looking at Trisha—"for little-boy waifs. If you could have seen your face that first summer you came here, Jord." Mrs. Adams shook her head in reminiscence, a smile deepening the curve of her mouth. "You reminded me of a banty rooster I had that summer. You were so determined to learn everything you needed to know to work on the farm. I think I knew then you'd be a man to reckon with someday."

Trisha could stand it no longer. "How can you call him a waif? His parents weren't exactly poor."

Her mother turned cool, blue eyes to her. "A waif is someone who doesn't have a home. And Jord didn't. Boarding school in the winter—shipped to his uncle in the summer. For his health," she added, the words heavy with contempt. Her eyes swung back to Jord. "It's a good thing I never met your mother. I'd have given her a piece of my mind."

Jord smiled. "I doubt if it would have done any good."

Trisha fought to keep her temper under control. Jord had always been a favorite of her mother's. Well aware of Diane's shortcomings, Mrs. Adams had refused to blame Jord for the dissolution of the marriage. Her mother simply had a blind spot where Jord was concerned. His charm was so potent that no matter how old a woman was, she was susceptible. Her mother was no exception. But to be fair, Jord had never given her mother any reason to think ill of him. He had always been particularly kind and considerate to the woman who had opened her home to him every summer.

"Well, if you two will excuse me, I think I'll retire to my room and read for a while and then go to bed. My back aches from picking all those peas."

"You work too hard, Ginny," Jord said softly.

She turned to look at him, her eyes glowing with fondness. "That's the way I'm made, Jord. I wouldn't know how to just sit down and rest. If there's anything you need, just ask. You know this is always your home."

Jord nodded. Trisha clenched her hands together under the bench until the short nails bit into her palms. Her mother was blind—blind—Mrs. Adams got to her feet and went to the downstairs bedroom that was hers.

Jord watched her go. After the door closed behind her, he turned to Trisha. "With your permission I'd like to take that black horse of yours out for a run."

Trisha hesitated and then nodded. She knew that Jord rode well. She had seen the four of them, Jord, Margie, Judson, and Diane, riding together often enough. She had been too young to be invited along.

He said, "I also need an alarm clock. I want to get a very early start tomorrow and do as much painting as I can in the cool of the morning. Do you have one I might borrow?"

Jamie piped up, "You can use mine."

Jord's lips tilted. "You have an alarm clock?"

Jamie nodded soberly. "It's blue with a little stem on top. Aunt Trisha said I would need it when I went to school this fall. She said if I was big enough to go to school, I was big enough to have my own clock. She's going to help me set and wind it and all that stuff."

Jord smiled. "Your Aunt Trisha is a smart lady. I'd like to borrow your clock—since you won't need it right now."

Jamie made a move as if to scurry away, but Jord caught his arm. "You can put it in my room, son."

Jolted, Trisha sent Jord a hot look. Jamie didn't see it. His face glowed with pleasure as he gazed up at Jord. "Okay."

The sound of Jamie's feet pounding up the stairs told her he was safely out of earshot. "You're asking for trouble," she told Jord. She avoided looking at him and instead began to clear the things from the table and carry them over to the sink. "He's beginning to like you a great deal."

"The feeling is mutual."

A nervous knot of anxiety twisted in her stomach. Jord had said he didn't want Jamie. Suppose he changed his mind?

She turned around and faced him, her color high. He insinuated himself everywhere, first with her mother and now with Jamie. "Look, why don't you just—go? You're getting close to Jamie now—but in another few days you'll fly off and leave him. He'll be hurt and disappointed."

"No," he said, shaking his head. "He'll forget me very quickly. Besides, I'm not staying here to get close to Jamie."

Driven, she cried, "Then why are you here?"

He stared at her in the quiet of the kitchen, his eyes glittering with some undefinable emotion. "I'm here," he said slowly, watching her, "to—attend Jamie's birthday party."

She stared back at him, her head high, her eyes flashing. "You're out of your mind." Quickly, to divert her thoughts from the painful channel they had taken, she turned her back to him and picked up Jamie's plate. "Margie called this afternoon. She wants to know if you would like to go to the square dance with them tomorrow night."

Jord frowned. "You're not going?"

"I—don't think so. Mother's on the refreshment committee, so she won't be home, and I haven't got a sitter for Jamie. The girl I usually get when Margie can't keep him will want to go to the dance, too."

"If that's the only thing that's keeping you home, I'll ask my assistant to come out and stay with him."

"Your—assistant?"

"Bradley Hunt. May I?" He gestured toward the phone, and she nodded.

Briefly Jord explained into the phone, and Trisha, listening, could see that Jord's asking Bradley Hunt was a mere formality. The man was in Jord's employ, but surely Jord didn't comandeer every hour of his day? Evidently he did, for after a few more words Jord cradled the telephone and said, "It's all set. Brad will be here tomorrow evening around eight o'clock." Disturbed by his straightforward yet unreadable gaze, she turned away and ran the water into the sink. As she added the soap she saw him step forward and pull the dish towel off the bar.

He picked up the first plate, and she tried to think of something to say, some light gambit of conversation to ease the tension between them, the electricity that seemed to gather in the air whenever they were alone together. But she couldn't. She had never been adept with words. Diane would not have fumbled for something to say. Diane was the vivacious one, the woman wise in the ways of men. She had admirers by the dozens while Trisha watched helplessly, knowing she could never emulate her sister's poise. No wonder Jord had fallen in love with her. Diane was the kind of girl Jord could marry and expect to fit into his life-style, a beautiful, sophisticated woman who could act as his hostess at corporate cocktail parties or sit beside him at the ballet. Jord had given her a place in his life as his wife. They had parted eventually, but the fact remained that Jord had loved Diane enough to marry her. The thought clawed at her throat, making her skin chill.

They finished in silence. He wiped the last plate, walked around her to place it in the cupboard, folded his towel, and hung it neatly on the rack. "I'll go out for that ride now."

"Just don't take any unnecessary chances with him, will you?"

"Are you worried about me—or your horse?" he asked, that glint of amusement sharpening, his lips twisting.

"The horse, naturally," she shot back at him, her chin lifting.

"Naturally," he echoed in an ironic tone and left her.

She had put Jamie to bed and taken her bath and was safely inside her room behind a closed door when Jord returned. She heard him making the small, familiar sounds of preparation for bed, and her mind's eye supplied the pictures, Jord stripping out of his clothes and climbing into the bathtub, his lean body glistening with moisture. She buried her head in the pillow and pulled it over her ears, hoping to stop those damnable thoughts from invading her mind.

The next morning it got hot immediately, as if the sun were promising no mercy for the next twelve hours. But because her mother had agreed to stay home to watch Jamie until two o'clock, Trisha decided she'd better walk the bean field to chop out weeds. The thoroughly unattractive job would at least take her away from the yard and out of the vision of Jord, who seemed to have painted nearly half of the south side of the barn before she was out of bed. The bean field was north of the house, on the other side of the grove, and very much out of visual range of the barn.

She wore jeans rather than shorts, because the bean leaves would cut across her thighs like sharp little knives if she didn't. It was better to suffer from the heat than endure that scraping. She made up for having to cover her legs by wearing a brief halter top that was little more than a red strip of material across her breasts anchored by a white string around her neck. She had long since turned a golden brown from neck to ankles and wouldn't need to guard against sunburn.

The plowed ground was rough walking. Bean plants, dark green and almost thigh high in places, seemed to stretch ahead of her endlessly. In minutes the perspiration began to trickle between her breasts, run down her back, and dampen her jeans along the backs of her thighs. She walked one round. The sun beat down on her head, heated her shoulders. She was thirsty. Her mother had given Jord the larger thermos, so Trisha had taken the smaller jug of water, thinking that it didn't matter, that in this heat she'd be thankful for an excuse to come back to the house early.

She forced herself to walk back into the field and begin on the

108

next two rows, hacking away with a long-handled hoe at the occasional cockleburs that seemed to defy all her efforts to get rid of them permanently. The volunteer corn had to be cut away, too, and she grasped its rough, thin leaves and chopped away at the roots. She completed the round before she allowed herself the first drink from the thermos.

An hour later she had walked three rounds and decided she had earned a small rest by the side of the grove and several long swallows from her thermos. She ducked under the shade of a tree and lifted the thermos to her lips. The water was cool and tasted heavenly. She had lifted it to indulge herself a second time when she heard the crack of a dry stick. Someone was walking through the grove toward her.

She waited in an almost intolerable suspense, knowing quite well that her mother would not be inclined to send Jamie out to the field in this heat.

Out of the shadow of the trees Jord emerged. He wore no shirt; his bare skin gleamed naked to the waist of his faded denims. A bright-red thermos swung in his hand.

As if he were the water she needed, she drank him in with her eyes, a heat beginning under her skin that had nothing to do with the sun.

"Your mother was worried about you. She asked me to bring you something else to drink."

The sight of him, his naked torso, the lean legs and thighs encased in denims as sweat-dampened as her own, his hair an antique gold in the sun, made words flee her brain. She extended her hand, but instead of handing the jug to her he caught hold of her wrist and pulled her toward him.

"You look very fetching in your work clothes," he said, his voice low and caught on the edge of huskiness. Had she ever thought his eyes cold? How wrong she had been. Slowly he let them roam over her, and those brown irises seemed to blaze with a fire that touched her already overheated skin like tongues of flame. "Just the way Daisy Mae might have looked—if she'd ever had to do a day's work."

From its journey to wherever it had gone, her voice returned to her throat. "Jord, let go of me."

"You're so warm, so soft . . ."

His hand tightened around her wrist, and he dropped the thermos. It fell to the earth with a muffled little clunk that seemed to reverberate in her ears. He drew her close, his eyes never leaving hers. She was powerless to stop him—even breathing seemed too much of an effort. He flattened his palm against the sensitive curve of her back, anchoring her hips in a suggestive position against his. Her pulses pounded, and she arched away, intolerably aware of how much his body betrayed his desire for her. But her slight resistance was useless; she seemed locked even more tightly against him. He bent his head, and she waited for what seemed like an endless eon of time, her eyes fastened on that full, attractive mouth. But her lips were not his destination. He bent lower, to that place between her breasts exactly where each curve formed a valley. His hair brushed her skin with a tantalizing lightness while, with infinite care, his tongue sought and found the droplet of perspiration trapped there. He licked it away gently, slowly, sensually cooling her skin and heating her blood all at the same time.

"Jord—" She couldn't move. Her arms were trapped under his. All she could do was cling to his belt and try to get some semblance of control over her reeling senses. But he was fast claiming her with his primitive caresses, moving his mouth intimately lower, pushing the red material away with ease, capturing and favoring a dark burgundy peak that was taut with response, bathing it in the erotic warmth of his mouth and tongue. Exhilarated with pleasure, she arched her back even more, allowing him easier access to her and pressing her hips more tightly against his. He rewarded her by favoring the other breast with the same, slow erotic attention of his tongue. She moaned his name, but he said nothing. It was as if he were seducing her with

110

his mind as well as with his mouth and hands, using some mysterious extrasensory perception to paint word pictures of those other, sweeter delights in store for her if she succumbed to his silent plea to let that delicious mouth discover every inch of her. She felt heady, light, as if she had no substance. And yet it was very real, this body of hers, and after years of deprivation she could no longer deny the desire that burned in a raging fire up through her.

Suddenly he thrust her away but maintained his hold on her arm. If he hadn't, she would have fallen with shock and surprise. "Jord—"

"My God! Do you have any idea what you do to me, woman? I wanted to take you, right now—here on the ground—"

He held her for a moment longer, his eyes still smoldering with the heat of his desire. Then he whipped his hand away, as if he could no longer bear to touch her, and thrust it up through his hair.

"I thought you weren't going to touch me again unless I asked you to," she shot back, her nerves singing with need that had been denied.

"Oh, you asked," Jord murmured. "Your eyes asked me to kiss you the moment I walked out of that grove."

She lost her temper in a glorious, pain-killing burst of anger. "Well, don't worry, Mr. Deverone. My eyes won't ask you again."

With a movement as quick as a snake he caught her wrist once more. "Don't tempt me to make you take that back."

"I'm not asking, I'm telling you to let go of me."

He shackled her wrist and dragged her to him. She struggled and pushed at him with her hands, but he grasped her at the nape and held her in a steel grip. "Be still."

He forced his mouth down on hers. He was angry, and his anger was heated by the passion of a moment ago. His whole body and mouth were bent to subjecting her to his domination. He was playing a new, cruel game he had never played before,

111

and she resisted and tried to twist away, pushing at him with her palms on his bare chest.

He ignored her strugglings for a moment, and then, suddenly, he eased that intolerable pressure. His mouth lifted away, only to return and take hers with a seductive, persuasive tenderness.

She had no defense against this embrace. It was the stuff of dreams, the tender giving of a man who is holding the woman he loves. His lips worshiped and caressed and teased and melted her resistance like snow in the sun, filled her with need, made her press closer to him and slip her hands around his neck. He responded by shifting his hold, one hand against the bare skin of her back at the waist, the other cupped over the curve of her bottom. She felt the heat rise in her, that untamed need to be one with him.

He loosened his hold slightly, and she could feel his muscles tightening to lift his head away. She uttered a strangled sound and clasped his neck at the nape, holding her mouth to his. He pushed her away and stepped back.

In one second she had gone from being locked in a loving embrace with him to staring at him from two feet away, as if he were an enemy she had consented to duel. She felt as though she had been through a time warp. Her breath rasped in her throat, her body cried out with pangs of deprivation, as if Jord's touch were a vital nutrient to her body.

For a long moment there in the blazing sun they stared at each other. All the things Jord might have said were in his eyes.

His lashes dropped, shielding that hard, contemptuous gleam from her. She flushed, knowing that he had proved her willingness to submit to him so clearly that he had no need to taunt her with it. He was perfectly willing to let her own wretched thoughts complete the punishment.

He bent slightly and reached for the jug that lay on the ground. "For you," he said, his voice bland. "In case you need something to cool you off."

*　*　*

112

She got through the rest of the day somehow. She was more than thankful for her mother's presence at the table during their noon meal. Her amiable conversation and Jamie's chatter provided a cover for her own silence. Jord seemed to ignore her, but once, when she got up to do her mother's bidding and refill his coffee cup, she leaned over to replace it in front of him and saw his eyes flash over her brief halter top and knew he was reminding her of his intimate exploration of what lay beneath.

When that hot, interminable afternoon was finally over, when she had walked nearly half the bean field with her mind replaying those moments in Jord's arms over and over again, she was more than ready to try to coax the sometime shower in the basement to work. That would accomplish a twofold purpose—cool her heated skin and make it possible for her to avoid Jord in the upper hallway.

The shower was working, and she stood underneath it, savoring the stream of tepid water pouring over her. She turned her face upward and let the cleansing liquid splash over her hot skin for several minutes. If only she could wash away the memory of Jord's touch as easily as she washed away the day's grime! But even now, as she thought of his mouth on her breasts, a tingle began at the base of her spine.

She had to stay away from him. The dancing would be old-fashioned eastern square dancing, but later on the band would play contemporary music. She had to stay out of Jord's arms—or she would betray how much she wanted to be in them. . . .

She almost hated to tie herself into her heavy terry robe, but that was a necessity. She didn't dare wrap her body in a towel and dash upstairs as she would have normally. The risk was too great.

She climbed the stairs and turned the corner to walk down the hallway. Jord was nowhere in sight. She slipped into her room with a feeling of relief and began to get ready.

Long ago on a shopping trip to Spencer she had purchased the outfit she planned to wear to the centennial dance. It was a western skirt, full and swingy with a ruffle around the bottom. The color was not the usual faded denim but a dusty rose. A white eyelet blouse with a wide ruffled neckline that she would wear off the shoulder went with the skirt, and around her waist she clipped a narrow silver belt with tiny chain tassels that dangled down next to one hip. It was too hot to wear western boots; instead she wore white strap sandals that wrapped just above her bare, slender ankles.

She heard Jord leave the bathroom and enter his room. She did her makeup slowly, thinking that he would leave his room before she finished. But even though she experimented with violet eyeshadow to highlight her eyes and dusted on a fine overlay of silver for night glamor, curled her lashes, and applied blusher on her cheeks and gloss on her lips, he still had not left his room when she was done. She gave her hair another complete brushing, letting its long, straight dark heaviness flow down her back. She had long ago given up trying to curl her hair. With careful cutting of the front to sweep across one side of her forehead, it had a shape of its own. In a dresser drawer she found a small silk rose the exact shade of her skirt and fastened it over her right ear.

She looked into the mirror and knew that she had never looked better. Her height, so long her despair, was just what was needed to carry off the double visual impact of ruffles above the breast and below the knee and the dramatic lines of the mid-calf skirt.

She could wait no longer. She would go down and perhaps be waiting in the living room when he came down. But as if he had been listening for the sound of her door, he stepped into the hallway at the exact same moment that she did.

Oh, God. She should have been prepared for the impact Jord would make in a cream silk western-cut shirt and smooth brown corded pants tucked into western boots, but she wasn't. From working out of doors his skin had turned to an even deeper brown, and the contrast of bronze flesh against cream silk made

114

her nerves begin that familiar oscillation. A dark-brown string tie was caught by a hammered silver slide that was obviously Navaho. In her mind she could see his brown fingers securing that fierce thunderbird on the brown silk at the hollow of his throat. Its predatory gaze suited him exactly. His blond hair had been changed by his days in the sun, too; it gleamed with highlights, and its gold strands were full, springy, brushed to perfection. The final assault of her senses was the smell of good male cologne that filled her nose.

The light in the hallway shone down on his sun-kissed hair and put a gleam in his eye. He examined her carefully, from the tiny rosebud in her hair to the airy sandals, his eyes returning to linger on the soft roundness of throat and shoulder exposed by the lowered neckline of her blouse. He raised his hand and, before she could move away, ran one long brown finger along the lace from her shoulder to the low, provocative point between the curve of her breasts. He began to caress her, his touch slow and erotic, devastatingly reminiscent of the way his tongue had begun that descent into the valley of her breasts that afternoon. "Is all this for the benefit of your current lover?"

"It's for no one's benefit but my own," she said huskily, unwilling to betray the storm his touch was creating by moving away. She was as acutely conscious of that light pressure as she might have been of the tip of a whip. "A woman feels better when she knows she looks good. She's more able to be at ease with everyone—women *and* men."

His lips curved upward. "I see." He gazed at her thoughtfully for a moment. "I rather think I liked you better as Daisy Mae." The fingertip went underneath the white cotton. He breathed in slightly, as if the discovery that she wore no bra was a shock to his senses. He recovered almost immediately and slowly, watching her face every second, probed sensually along one rounded upthrust curve.

She stood utterly still and gazed at him, forcing her body to be rigid, overwhelmingly aware that every leaping nerve within

115

her was screaming to press closer, to allow that warm hand to cup the full weight of her breast. But she couldn't. She couldn't let him do this to her, devastate her with his touch and his evocative words. She would convince him that his touch left her cold no matter how much her body cried otherwise.

She stood unflinching, her face set. His eyes locked with hers, and a slight smile lifted his lips, but those dark-brown irises glowed with desire. With a soft little laugh in the depth of his throat he bent his head and placed his lips lightly over hers.

The double onslaught of his mouth and hands broke down the last of her fragile defenses. She moved backward. "Don't." The breathlessness of the short, clipped word gave her away.

He laughed again, a soft sound of triumph. "Save a dance for me," he murmured.

"No." She glared at him, her cheeks no longer needing the artifice of blusher.

Without touching her he leaned forward and once more brushed his lips over hers. Then, before she could react, he turned his back and walked down the hallway.

Her heart pounded as he turned the corner and gazed at her from the opposite end of the hall. "You will," he mocked and began to descend the stairs, his head disappearing below the bannister.

She clenched her fists and stood there, waiting for him to reach the bottom of the stairs.

Bradley Hunt arrived shortly after she walked into the living room, and his presence lightened the atmosphere. Trisha liked him almost at once; good humor shone out of his eyes. The feeling seemed to be mutual. Brad's eyes were openly admiring as she gave him the pertinent instructions. For her part she had no qualms about leaving Jamie with him. By the time Judson and Margie arrived, Brad had Jamie involved in a competitive game of Fish.

Judson was not so easily satisfied. The greetings had been cool between the two men, and when the four of them were in the car,

Judson hesitated for a moment before starting the engine. Then he twisted around to face Jord and Trisha in the back seat. "Are you sure this guy is okay?"

Trisha opened her mouth, but Jord put a restraining hand on her wrist. The shock of contact with him took the words from her throat.

"He's worked with me closely for the last six years. I think I can vouch for his integrity." The words were soft, guarded.

"Well, you'd better." Judson was oddly belligerent. "These days there are a lot of nutty people running around."

The silence in the car was oppressive. Even Margie seemed stricken by it.

Jord's voice hardened. "Do you think I'm so irresponsible I'd leave my—son with just anyone?" There was hard contempt in every word.

A dull flush crept into Judson's face and colored the back of his neck. "No, I suppose you wouldn't." His head swiveled around, a hand reached forward, and the engine roared into life.

CHAPTER SIX

The tension between the two men did not ease in the ten minutes it took to drive to Arien. Judson's mouth was still tight with anger when the four of them walked into the high-school gym.

Red, white, and blue streamers were strung from the rafters to a point on the wall below. The stage curtain was open, and a gigantic enlarged photo showing Arien as it had looked a hundred years ago with buggies tied to hitching posts and two buildings on a treeless street was mounted behind the five members of the western-country band, who were readying themselves to play. The floor was golden with a new coat of wax. Round tables and chairs sat around the walls, and a huge circulating fan lifted the red paper tablecloths that were anchored only by blue hurricane lamps. Trisha saw her mother bending over to light one at the far end of the room.

"You'll buy a lottery ticket, won't   Judson?" Eleanor Jackson, a comely woman in her late fifties, asked as they walked through the door. "Jord! How nice to see you."

Jord greeted her politely. "It's good to be here, Eleanor. How have you been?"

After she had told him how she was, Jord asked after her

118

married daughters, and she gave him a quick run down of their lives in two cities at opposite ends of the country. Eleanor Jackson was no more immune to his charm than any other woman.

Trisha turned away—to find Loren's sister, Honey McAllister, gazing at Jord. Slightly younger than Trisha, the girl was an attractive pixie with a Texas drawl who worked in one of the cafés in Spencer. She took a great deal of teasing about her Texas accent, but she was good-natured about it and had learned to combat it with a dazzling smile.

"Hello, Trisha." The message in her eyes was entirely different. The McAllister family had moved to Iowa from Texas just two years ago, long after Jord had stopped making his yearly visits, which made Jord a new, exciting stranger to Honey. Her eyes traveled avidly up and down his lean form, then turned to Trisha. *Introduce me,* she implored with her glance, as clearly as if she were shouting it. Unlike Trisha, she was dressed in a short dressy dress in a warm brown color with a V neckline that exposed her tanned skin and the beginnings of her small breasts. Her long caramel-colored hair curled over her bare shoulders.

Trisha performed the introductions in a cool voice. Jord smiled and took Honey's hand. He inspected her gravely. "Is that a touch of Texas I hear in your voice?"

"You bet," Honey answered pertly. "And I'm proud of it."

Jord smiled. "I thought Texas was noted for bigness. Looks as if the state can produce nice things in small packages, too." He held her hand, and she colored attractively. "Why, thank you, sir. That's right kind of you."

"Not at all," Jord murmured, still holding Honey's hand.

Trisha had vowed to pawn him off on the first available female she saw, but Honey McAllister was not the one she would have chosen. They went on talking, as if they had known each other for ages, and when Honey invited Jord to sit at her table since Trisha would be there with Loren, and Jord turned to her and said blandly, "Is that all right with you?" she was perversely, gloriously angry. But all she could do was swallow that furious lump in her throat and say coolly, "Yes, of course."

Honey turned big, brown eyes to Trisha. "Loren will be here a little later, Trisha. He's counting on sitting with you."

Trisha gave her a mocking little nod. "Great."

Fuming, she followed Honey to a table well back against the wall but directly across from the stage. The view was excellent, but the table was more private than those toward the front.

"Sit here, Jord," Honey invited, pulling out a chair for him. She kept a firm grip on it and pushed it forward as he sat down.

He said lazily, watching Honey as she and Trisha seated themselves, "Is that a Texas welcome—or an Iowa one?"

"Some of both, I reckon. Where are you from, Jord?"

"New York City."

"Must be quite a change for you, coming to our quiet little town. What brings you here?" Honey leaned forward and put her arms on the table so that she could look more easily into Jord's face.

"Family business."

Trisha didn't think it was possible for Honey's smile to increase in voltage, but it did. "Are you and Trisha related?"

"Not by blood. I'm her brother-in-law's cousin." A smile lifted Jord's mouth.

"You're Judson's cousin? Yes, I can see the family resemblance now." Honey turned to Trisha. "You never told me about your big-city, shirttail relation."

Coolly Trisha said, "Jord is Jamie's father."

Honey's eyebrows flew up. "Now I remember."

The band began to play, and conversation was no longer possible, something for which Trisha was profoundly grateful, until she saw Honey slant her gorgeous eyes up to Jord and say with a mischievous glint, "Think a big-city man can dive for the oyster and duck for the clam?"

"I might be able to," Jord drawled. "If I had the right instruction."

"Come on, then, and dance with me. It's real simple, just like the Virginia Reel, mostly follow the leader. You'll catch on."

Jord rose, his hand finding the back of Honey's tiny waist. "Lead the way."

Trisha tried not to watch them dancing, but it was almost impossible to direct her eyes away from the delicately built girl and the tall man, who handled her as if she were fragile blown glass. When it came their turn to slide down the middle and swing each man and woman in the line, Honey's face looked as if it were lit from within by a fire glow.

"I've been looking all over for you. How long have you been sitting here?"

Loren McAllister slid into the chair beside her. There was a tiny nick in his chin where he had cut himself shaving.

"Not too long." He leaned forward to press his lips against her cheek, and she had to stop herself from shrinking away from his moist mouth. Like Honey, Loren was thin, but unlike her, he was tall, just tall enough to match Trisha's height. His narrow face had a pinched look about it tonight, and she supposed he was displeased because his father had made him finish taking care of the cattle on the farm before he could get away for the evening. It was a constant source of irritation to Loren, who felt that a man of his age should have more to say about the farming operation. Privately Trisha agreed.

"Who's that out there dancing with Honey?"

She told him. He frowned. "He's staying at your house?"

"Yes."

"I'm not sure I like that, Trisha."

"I don't see that you have any say in the matter, Loren, one way or another." Gently spoken, the words were tinged with frost.

"Of course I have a say. After all, we are practically engaged —" Just at that moment the band stopped playing, and Loren's voice seemed to shout out into the silence. People turned and stared at them both.

Someone shouted, "That a way, Loren. Go get 'em, tiger," and someone else whistled. They all knew of Loren's long pursuit.

He looked around him, his face getting redder. There was general laughter, and then he grinned sheepishly and looked away from Trisha to the watching crowd and announced in his broad Texas drawl, "Well, it's time you all knew, anyway."

"Loren, don't," she muttered under her breath.

Loren kept his brilliant smile pinned on his face and said in a low, warning tone, "Now you'll have to say yes, won't you?" He smiled and nodded at people, his voice coming out between gritted teeth. "Because the whole town already thinks you have."

Honey came back to the table, holding Jord's hand. "Well, congratulations, brother. It's about time." She leaned down and kissed him and then walked around to Trisha and hugged her. "We've been wondering just when our slowpoke brother was going to get around to admitting to you that he loved you. Welcome to our family, Trish."

Panicked, she looked up into Jord's face. It was impassive, glacial.

Loren insisted she dance with him for rest of the night, and while they danced she received teasing comments from everyone on the floor. The entire evening was a nightmare that seemed to have no end. And the worst part of the nightmare was that she was tempted, severely tempted to let the bogus engagement continue and evolve into a bogus marriage. Dear God! She couldn't use Loren to ease the loss of Jord—a loss that was inevitable.

When the band began to play contemporary music, and the dancers broke from their long lines to become gyrating couples, Trisha managed to escape Loren and edge out of one of the side doors that had been left open for coolness. She walked quickly away from the crowded room into the night air, loving the feel of the breeze on her face. At the far end of the yard there was a tree she used to play under, and she headed for that now. As she reached the tree she saw a man step away from the trunk, the tip of a glowing cigarette in his hand. The moonlight illuminated his gold hair, and for a moment her heart seemed to jump up to an uncomfortable spot in her throat. Then she realized she had been mistaken. It was not Jord who stood under the shade of the elm, smoking. It was Judson Adams.

"Hello, Trisha. How are you holding up?"

She made a choked sound. She had been hoping that the grounds were deserted, that she could drop that plastic smile she had fixed to her face. "Don't ask."

"It's been rough, has it?

Out of the darkness his voice sounded so kind, so understanding that the control she had been clinging to deathlessly all evening deserted her. She twisted away from him and buried her face in her hands, letting the mask dissolve, letting the nervous tremors course through her body. She wasn't crying—but she was very close to it.

"My darling girl! Don't do this to yourself." He turned her around and with one finger under her chin raised her face to the moonlight. "You don't—you aren't having his child, are you?" he asked gently.

It was such a ludicrous idea that a laugh came bubbling up through her tight throat. "No."

"Then what is it? Aren't you in love with him?"

She shook her head. "It's all a mistake." At his slight grimace she went on, "I know all I have to do is tell him no at the end of the evening. It's just that—now there's been so much damage done. There'll be talk about me—and mother will hate that." She shuddered and turned away, a choked sound of distress escaping despite her pride-bound control.

Judson flung his cigarette away in a wide, glowing arc, and in the next moment she felt his warm arms encircle her. "Don't, honey, please don't."

The unfamiliar feeling of being in Judson's arms made her stiffen, and then his physical likeness to Jord made her forget who he was. Her imagination soared. It might have been Jord standing there, holding her, comforting her. . . . She clutched his back and clung to him, her voice still shaking, on the edge of despair. "I can't bear to think of going through what we went through when Diane—"

He froze, as if her words had sent their own little dagger into his side. Then the tenseness ebbed, and he took hold of her upper arms and held her away to look down into her face. "Trisha." There was a low, throbbing note in his voice. "You're making something out of nothing. If you don't want to marry him, you won't, that's all. It was a stupid thing for any man to do, announce to an entire community an engagement he hadn't bothered to check out with his fiancée. It will be talked about, sure, but it will all blow over. They'll forget and go on to the next topic of conversation."

She stood in his arms, and the feeling of being with Jord faded. This was Judson, her stepbrother, and his was the voice of reason. He had not really been a brother to her when she was younger—there was too much of an age gap between them, and Judson had exhibited only a casual interest in her; but tonight she found his concern for her touching.

She raised her face to him. "Jud—I—" She stopped, unable to say the things that were hovering over her tongue, unable to tell him how she wished she knew him better and had been able to comfort him during that gray year he and Margie had lost their child and learned that they wouldn't have another.

She didn't have to say the words. He looked down at her moon-silvered face and said, "I know, honey, I know. We've missed a lot not knowing each other, haven't we?" He bent his head and touched his lips to her forehead lightly. It was a kiss such as Simon might have given her years ago.

The whispery sound of grass being pressed under a booted foot was the first warning they had that they were no longer alone.

"This is a cozy little scene."

Irrationally she gave a guilty start and turned. Jord Deverone's voice was as recognizable as his cream silk shirt. Judson's arm tightened protectively around her waist, locking her to his side.

"Go away, Deverone," Judson retorted, his voice equally harsh. "You're not wanted here."

"I don't imagine I am." Even in the moonlight she could see the hard planes of his face, the proud lift of his head, the way the moon streaked his golden hair. "Some things never change, do they?"

An odd little silence followed his words. Trisha's stomach tightened, a thousand butterflies climbing at the walls. What was he talking about? Was he accusing them of having an affair—and Judson of having done this before? She couldn't let him think those vile things about Jud—Jud who had been concerned for her happiness. She said, "Jord, don't! You don't know what you're talking about. We were just talking—"

"You have a strange way of talking to a man." He took another step toward her. "From where I stood it looked like a touching little love scene."

"Well, it wasn't," Trisha said flatly. "I won't have you thinking that of Jud—"

Jord's nostrils seemed to flare, as if he were a wild animal scenting trouble in the wind. "If you want one last fling before you're married—have it with me."

"Don't you dare proposition her." Judson tightened his grip on Trisha. She didn't move. She could feel the coiled tension in every muscle of Judson's body. The two men were the same height, but there was a hard tone in Jord's body that Judson, sitting on a tractor all day and doing much of his work with mechanical aids, did not have. If Judson were hurt, Margie would be devastated. "Stop this, both of you."

They ignored her.

"Why shouldn't I proposition her?" Jord said evenly. "You are."

"I'm warning you—" Judson got out between clenched teeth.

"Threats are a waste of everyone's time. What really counts

is action." Jord tipped his head to one side, as if he were thinking. "We could, as you suggested a few days ago, settle our differences in the barn. But what then? Does the winner take all?" He let his eyes roam leisurely over Trisha, making it clear what he considered to be "all."

"This whole thing is ridiculous," she said hotly. "There's nothing between Jud and me—"

"Or," Jord went on, as if he hadn't heard her, "we can make a horse trade. You have something I want"—Jord paused—"and I have something you want."

"Nothing you have interests me," Judson said coldly.

"Except Jamie."

The night breeze stirred, and the leaves rustled.

"I'll trade you," Jord said softly. "Trisha—for Jamie."

Trisha cried, "No—" and Judson's fingers tightened, biting into her skin.

"You bastard. You don't have the right to bargain with my son's life. He belongs to me—"

Trisha's gasp stopped his flow of words.

He let go of her. She might have lost her balance if Jord hadn't stepped forward and caught her arm.

In the long aching silence the dark night seemed to reel around her, tilting itself like a house of mirrors. Truth and lies, fact and illusion. There was ringing conviction in Judson's voice; she knew he spoke the truth. But how could it be? For years she had believed Jamie was Jord's son. Now she knew he wasn't. He was Judson's son. She stared at him, the man she had thought loved Margie.

The moon illuminated his strained face. "Trisha. I'm sorry. I—never wanted you to know."

"I—can't believe it." Her whispered words seemed to blend with the breeze.

"It's true," he admitted in a low, tortured tone. "I wanted to marry Diane from the very first time I saw her. But she didn't want to stay here. She wanted me to sell my land and move to

126

the city." He swallowed and went on as if he had a dire need to share his anguish. "I couldn't do it. I belong here—nowhere else." He raised his head. "When Margie lost the baby, she—shut me out. And Diane came home for a vacation." He shrugged. "I was—lonely; Diane was on the rebound from a love affair. We found solace for our wounded egos with each other. We comforted each other." He sighed. "And the inevitable happened." He clenched his jaw and said harshly, "I knew it was wrong. But I needed her. And I think—she needed me. She knew I wanted children. That's why she had Jamie. She was sure I'd leave the farm if she had my child. But I—couldn't do it. I couldn't leave Margie. Diane was furious. She told me she'd see to it that I would watch Jamie grow up and know that I could never claim him, never tell the world that he was my son." He shook his head. "She wanted revenge—and she got it. Years of it." His voice broke.

"Jud, don't." She laid her hand on his arm—and felt the support of Jord's leave her. "You did the right thing. You stayed with Margie."

"I love her," he said fiercely. "I realize now what I had with Diane was like a—a sickness. After our affair I was cured. But then there was Jamie." His tone roughened. "He's my son. Jord knew she was carrying my child when he married her. There's no question about his paternity."

"No," Jord said softly. "There's no question about his paternity."

The words sent a singing elation through her veins that she shouldn't have felt. But still—Jord was not the kind of man who would voluntarily marry a woman who carried another man's child. He had too much pride, too much arrogance. She asked him coolly, "I thought you loved her. If you knew, why did you marry her?"

"The world may be more liberal today, but I knew how your mother would feel. I didn't want Virginia's grandchild born out of wedlock," he said simply. "When Diane gave me the opportunity to prevent that, I took it."

She wanted to believe him. But she couldn't. "You can't expect me to believe you rearranged your whole life just to prevent some spiteful gossip from reaching my mother's ears."

In the darkness, his eyes burned. "You don't understand that, do you? Well, why should you? You had a mother who managed to provide a stable, loving environment for you through the death of her husband and her remarriage. I wasn't so lucky. You can't have any idea what it's like to be brought up feeling like there's nothing behind you but a gaping, black hole, and if something happens, you'll fall into it. And like a lot of teenage boys, I found all the wrong outlets for my nervous energy. Why do you think my mother and father sent me out to the country every summer?" The question was directed at Trisha, but she didn't answer.

As if once the floodgates were open, he couldn't close them, Jord went on. "Because I'd been in trouble, and they didn't know how to deal with me. I was very close to becoming a juvenile deliquent, and they didn't want to bother with me, so they did with me what they did with all the problems in their life they couldn't handle—they got me out of their sight." He stopped as if aware that he had revealed far more of himself than he had intended. "Virginia took me into her home and showed me another way of living; the way people lived together as a *real* family. She healed me and taught me, with her warmth and understanding. I would even fantasize that I was really part of your family," he confessed, "and that Virginia was really my mother. All those summers. It was so easy to come here. And so hard to go." In a low flat tone he said, "When I found out about Diane, I would have done anything to spare your mother the pain of learning the truth, of having to live with it in this small town. And then there were you and Margie to consider." He drew in a breath, his voice a deep, husky whisper when he finally continued. "I was given so much. I didn't think that

128

giving Diane's child a name was too great a price to pay in exchange."

Trisha's heart leapt in wild elation. He had tried to tell her, but she had refused to listen. That first afternoon in the barn and so many other times. What a stupid, stubborn fool she had been not to hear him out, to trust him. He had never loved Diane.

Jord shifted his gaze to Judson. "My offer still stands."

Her joy in the truth she'd just learned vanished. He was going to persist in his ridiculous assumption that she was involved with Judson. But he couldn't possibly be serious about this . . . bargain.

Judson's protest was flat, harsh. "There's nothing between Trish and me."

"Yes—or no?" Jord repeated, the words like steel against flint.

In an appeal for reason Judson cried, "I can't bargain with something I don't have, man."

Jord turned to her. "What about you," he asked softly. "Are you willing to bargain with something you don't have—yet?"

The temptation was strong to tell him what he could do with his bargain and walk away. But she couldn't do it. Jord had offered to give Judson his son. She couldn't let Judson refuse the one opportunity he might ever have to get Jamie. He had suffered enough. But—if she said yes, it would be as good as admitting to Jord that she loved Judson. And she would lose him forever. It was so simple, so clear cut. She could stay silent, and not run the risk of having Jord think she was involved with Judson—or she could give Jamie to Judson, and lose whatever affection and respect Jord had for her. The silence echoed on into the night, deepening, swelling.

Then she lifted her head and said clearly, "All right. I—agree." The cool, clear voice dropped into the silence like the tinkle of glass.

Jord was utterly still, his face like a dark mask, his body stone. "I'll tell Brad to begin the paper work tomorrow. Do you have a lawyer?"

"Yes, Conrad Martin. Trisha, don't be a fool. We'll think of something else."

"Is he in Emmetsburg?" Jord continued relentlessly.

Distracted, Judson said, "Yes—yes. For God's sake, man, don't do this."

"I'll have Brad contact him first thing in the morning."

"Trisha, tell him no. You know as well as I do that there's nothing between us."

She turned to him, still not believing Jord could actually be serious. "As you say, there's nothing between us." Something of her meaning must have penetrated. He gave her a long, hard look. She made her meaning clearer. "But as long as Mr. Deverone is determined to give us something for nothing, we'd be foolish not to take him up on his offer."

Judson turned to Jord, his face twisted. "Dammit, man, see some reason. There must be another way . . ."

"No," Jord said implacably. Then his voice softened. "Diane's not the only one who can be vindictive. If you don't agree to stay away from Trisha, I'll—take Jamie with me when I go." His eyes never left Trisha's face. His mouth was hard.

Dear God! The man had no heart, no soul. If he had ever really loved one woman in his life, that woman was her own mother. He had married Diane to protect her, and now he was doing it again, using any means to avert another possibly disastrous situation for a woman he cared for passionately. "There isn't any need to threaten us, Jord," she said coldly. "We've already agreed to your terms."

"You have. My cousin hasn't."

"No, dammit. No!" Judson raked a hand through his hair. "Anyway, there is still—Diane. She would never agree to letting me adopt him, I know she wouldn't."

"If you agree to my terms, I'll deliver her written permission to you along with mine," Jord said blandly.

Angrily Judson turned on him. "How are you going to accomplish that miracle? Have you got a way of blackmailing Diane, too?"

Jord's voice was cold. "Actually, yes. Diane gets a monthly income from me. I don't think she'd be happy to lose it."

Judson made an anguished sound. Trisha could see that he was thinking, thinking about having Jamie as his own, with the obstacle of Diane removed. At last he groaned, "For God's sake, I can't—can't let him go. I agree."

The breeze freshened, and it whispered through her hair, rippling the black silky weight of it around her shoulders. She lifted her head to look at Jord.

He watched her, waited to see her reaction to Judson's words. She met those brown eyes straight on, her pride stiffening her spine, her violet eyes glittering, willing him to see that he was wrong, that she wasn't interested in Judson as a lover. She waited, hoping, her breath held.

Not a flicker of understanding softened that hard, cold face, that firm mouth. His eyes moved over her dispassionately and then seemed to look directly through her, as if he hadn't the slightest interest in what he was seeing.

For Jord she no longer existed. He believed she was in love with her sister's husband; her own agreement to Jord's bargain had condemned her in his eyes. He would never believe in her innocence. A cold chill feathered over her arms and settled somewhere in the region of her heart. Her skin felt icy, her face hot.

She turned away, her hand at her middle. She felt sick, desolated. She knew, without being told, that never again would Jord hold her, touch her, kiss her. She felt as if she had sustained a severe body blow. Her throat tightened, her stomach clenched. She used every scrap of pride, every ounce of will to hide the state of her emotions. But all the while her mind was crying, *Why? Why now? Why did you pick this precise moment, when it's evident to an idiot how little he trusts you and how much he despises you—to realize that you love him?*

131

In one stroke she had lost Jord—and Jamie. Her knees shook. For one horrible moment she thought her teeth would chatter. She had to get away. Wordlessly she pivoted and began to walk over the grass toward the schoolhouse. She had gone three steps when a tuft of grass caught at her toe. She stumbled and almost fell. No one came to help her. Alone, she regained her balance and kept walking.

The brightness of the gym was almost a shock to her system. She blinked, trying to clear her eyes. She was met with knowing smiles and glances. She circled around the room, her answering smile wooden. Loren was standing beside the refreshment table, talking to Jennifer Lang, leaning over the tall bouquet of red and white carnations. Their spicy smell was pleasing, but the odor of the finger sandwiches and mints and nuts was faintly nauseating.

Jennifer raised sad brown eyes to Trisha. "I was just congratulating Loren on his engagement." There was a wistful envy in every word. Trisha felt a sharp impatience. Were all men such blind fools? Jennifer adored Loren. And she would make the perfect wife for him. She was gentle and kind and unaffected by the restless need for the love of another man that plagued Trisha.

"Where have you been?" Loren frowned, as if she were a puzzle he couldn't quite work out. "I've been looking all over for you."

"I just stepped out for a breath of fresh air. Loren, would you mind very much taking me home?"

"Now? But it's only midnight. I—asked Jennifer to dance—"

"Then let me have your car," she said quickly. "You can ride home with Honey."

"I'll take you home," he said grudgingly, and she would have protested, but she knew she had to talk to him, and perhaps afterward he could return to the party—and dance with Jennifer.

He was quiet on the way home, but instead of turning the corner that would take them to the road to her home, he went the opposite way, around the lake.

132

"What are you doing?" Trisha turned to look at him.

There was a hardness about his mouth that she had never seen before.

"I thought I'd look at the lake for a while with my fiancée," he said grimly, "before she tells me to go jump in it."

"Loren—"

He shook his head and stepped down on the accelerator. "Don't say it. Not yet."

He turned onto the road that led to a little-used park, and stopped the car on a small rise that overlooked the water. He cut the engine and hunched back into the seat. He did not look at her. "Okay," he said. "Say it. And for God's sake don't tell me you're not right for me. Just say it clearly and simply, something you should have said months ago. Loren, I don't want to marry you."

She put her hand on his arm, and he snatched it away, as if her touch was intolerable. "You're not making this easy for me," she said.

He turned to look at her, and even though she couldn't see his eyes in the darkness, she knew they blazed with emotion. "I don't want to make it easy for you," he said huskily. "I want to make it as hard for you as I possibly can."

"Please—don't," she breathed, thinking that she knew exactly how he felt. She, too, had been rejected by the one she loved. She clenched her hands in her lap to keep from reaching out to him again. "Loren, I know how you feel, I really do. It's just that— well, how honest would it be for me to marry you—feeling as I do? We'd only end up more miserable."

"We both like the same things," he said, his voice belligerent, like a little boy who's been told he can't have an ice cream cone. "We both like the country."

"It's not enough," she said softly. "There has to be more than that."

He gripped the wheel with both hands, the tendons taut under

133

the skin. "If I were different," he said grittily. "If I were more like that city dude—"

"Loren, don't," she said huskily. "Don't you see? It isn't you who needs to be different. It's me." She paused. "You'll find another woman, one who loves you and wants you exactly as you are"—she took a breath and smiled, a faint teasing in her voice—"Texas accent and all."

He sat quietly, as if he were absorbing her words. Ahead of them the water shimmered a dark slate. A slip of a cloud passed over the moon and then was gone. She had opened the car window, and the wind lifted the white eyelet ruffle on her blouse.

"I'd like to go home now," she said gently. "Why don't you go back to the dance, Loren?" She waited a beat of time. "Jennifer Lang will be disappointed if you don't."

He loosened his grip on the wheel and leaned forward to start the car in a sudden quick move. "Maybe I will," he said half-defiantly.

The gray car in the yard reminded her that Jord's assistant was still in the house. She told Loren good-bye and slid from the car. When he moved to get out, she said, "No, don't walk me to the door, there's no need."

He hesitated for a moment and then drawled, "No, I suppose there isn't."

She shut the car door and half-ran up the sidewalk. Loren revved the car and spun gravel as he tore away, leaving her to walk into the house alone, feeling a strange mixture of sadness and relief.

"Back so soon?" Brad Hunt was reading in the living room, looking almost as if he belonged there with the newspaper scattered at his stockinged feet.

"Yes. I got—tired. Was he good for you?"

"We got along fine. He's a good kid."

"Would you like some coffee or anything?"

She half-hoped he would refuse. Instead he grinned, stuck a dark-stockinged toe out to probe for a shoe, and said, "Sure."

134

She braced herself for another hour of pretending, another hour of speaking, moving, responding. She couldn't have said afterward what they talked about. Movies, books, people. Nothing about Jord. Nothing about the ache in her heart. Nothing about the destruction of her life in the simple space of twenty minutes. Nothing of any importance.

He left at last, and she climbed the stairs. She was bone-tired. But when she undressed and got into bed, she couldn't sleep. She spent a restless two hours—waiting. It was hot. She got up and opened the window and her door. The south breeze swirled through the room, but as she lay back down in bed the thoughts that went around inside her head created more heat inside her body. As if that were not enough, it was Honey's car that brought Jord to her doorstep. Shamelessly she got up out of bed and saw him helping the petite woman out of the car. Honey walked him to the door. Trisha shrank away from the window and got back into bed, but the front door was directly below her window, and she could hear the whispered murmurs, Honey's appealing husky drawl mingling with Jord's low attractive voice —followed by the silence that told her more clearly than words that Jord was kissing Honey good night.

She lay there, sick, angry, and jealous. Like a tantalizing ghost, the memory of Jord's mouth on her throat filled her senses. Was he pressing kisses along Honey's throat, teasing her skin with his mouth?

Honey made a smothered sound and then giggled softly and said, "Night, Jord. Call me now, you hear?"

She couldn't imagine giggling in Jord's arms. His mouth didn't amuse. It devastated, destroyed. She twisted in the bed, kicking aside the sheet, and then forced herself to lie rock still, shut her eyes and simulate the deep breathing of sleep as she heard Jord's step on the stairs.

A hand clamped down on the wrist of the arm she had thrown over her head. She cried out in terror. Her eyes flew open—and she saw him then, the dark, dangerous shadow that was Jord. He was leaning over her.

"Don't try to pretend you were sleeping," Jord murmured silkily. He sat down on the bed, keeping his shackling hold on her wrist.

"Get out of here," she whispered, somehow through her shock and alarm remembering Jamie. "You and I have nothing to say to each other."

"But that's where you're wrong, darling," he murmured. "Now that you've broken your engagement, we have more to say to each other than ever."

"You—know?" She stared up at him, trying to see the expression on his face. All she saw was a mask of hard skin and bone and the uncompromising line of his jaw.

"I have to give your disconsolate swain credit," he said, leaning back as if he were settling in. "He came back to the dance and spent the rest of the evening looking quite happy to have young Jennifer console him."

"I—I'm glad."

"I'm sure you are," he said softly. "It makes what we're about to do much—less complicated."

He leaned forward, and before she could dodge away, he brushed his mouth lightly over hers. That light touch of his lips was like a wonderful gift. She had been certain she would never feel the touch of that warm, exciting mouth again. . . .

His lips tantalized her, nibbled at hers. The light caressing seemed to melt her bones, make her want to relax back into the pillows and let him go on making love to her. But she couldn't do that. "Jord, no, don't do this."

"Why not?" He was discovering the soft skin of her throat, the sensitive curve that was visible above the square-cut neckline of her shorty pajamas. "You want it—and so do I." He released her wrist. His hands went to the bottom of her short sleep garment. He lifted her with one hand and stripped it away from her with the other.

136

A cool breeze touched her breasts, and in the next instant Jord leaned forward and took a taut peak into his mouth. An explosion of desire shook her. "Jord—don't." But her hands were stroking his head, urging him to continue the lovely agony. He laughed softly and ignored her protest. His hands went on playing over her, discovering her.

"All curves and softness and circles, aren't you, darling?" He traced around the circumference of each breast and then discovered the much tinier circle of each taut peak. When she was gasping with pleasure, his tongue followed the exact path of his hand. Then his tongue took possession of her navel, erotically claiming the place that had once been her source of life.

She was beyond protest, beyond the ability to think of anything except that this was Jord, the man she loved, and that being with him was a thousand times more exciting than her dreams of him. To her he was the perfect lover, patient, gentle—and expert.

His hand wandered lower. He lifted her hips and divested her of her last garment.

She made a soft sound of protest. It was the final barrier he had allowed her to keep against him, and now that was gone. He stroked her silken thigh. "Long lovely legs," he murmured. "They're beautiful." He brushed his mouth over the tanned satiny skin. His hand stroked her, found the sweetness of her femininity. "Jord." Her voice was low and tortured and brought a low laugh to his lips. "Do you want me very badly, Trisha?"

"Yes. Yes, Jord. I want you. I always have—"

His hand stilled. He reached up and grasped her bare shoulders. "Don't lie to me." His voice was harsh, rasping. "We'll keep this honest, at least. I've cheated you out of having a love affair with the man you want. But you're willing to take me as a substitute. All right. I accept that. And I'm more than willing to play the part. But don't compound the lie by pretending that you care for me." His hand went to his shirt and he began to unbutton the buttons.

She shivered uncontrollably. He despised her. He was going to make love to her, take her—but it meant nothing to him.

She fended off his hands. Steeling herself, feeling as if she were bleeding to death inside, she said, "I'm sorry, Jord. I—can't. I have to have some illusion." Then pride and anger and bitter disillusion made her lift her chin and say, "Judson was kind and considerate." That was true, as far as it went. She had to get him out of this room before she broke down and cried, before she told him the truth, that she loved him and needed him desperately. . . . She swallowed and told the most blatant lie of all. "Do you really want me to lie in your arms pretending it's Judson making love to me?" The words almost choked her, but she forced herself to go on. "I thought you had too much pride to—stand in for Judson the second time around."

Even in the dark she could feel the fury in those dark eyes. "You were lying about not loving him, weren't you?"

"Yes." *Not then, now!*

The silence seemed to ring in her ears. It was as if the night played a song that she couldn't hear.

He got up from the bed, and the shift of its softness under her and the sudden coolness where his hip had rested against hers left her desolate.

"You're right," he said, his voice hard and cold. "I don't want another woman who imagines herself in love with Jud. One was enough."

His step was soft as he walked the short distance from her room to his. She heard him undressing, and the soft creak of the bed under his weight. He was so close—and he had never been further out of her reach.

She got out of bed and groped around in the dark for her pajamas, feeling as if nothing in her life would matter after this night. She got into her night clothes and lay back down, knowing that sleep was impossible. She stared into the dark, watching the moon move across the sky, wishing she were on it.

* * *

"Sleep well?" Jord taunted the next morning at breakfast. She had tried to cover the dark circles with makeup, but she knew she had only partially succeeded.

"It's the heat," she countered and set a plate of scrambled eggs and toast in front of Jamie.

"Is it?" he murmured. Jord's lips lifted at the quick use of the weather as an excuse for her limp look.

She turned her back on him and went to the stove to pick up the coffeepot. She desperately wished she could see some sign of disturbance in Jord's lean figure relaxing lazily in the breakfast nook. But of course she couldn't. He was cool and poised and— contemptuous. She turned, the coffeepot in her hand. His eyes swept lazily over her, from her black, straight hair tied back in a red ribbon down past the red halter top and the bare skin of her midriff to the faded jeans that clung to her stomach and thighs. His mouth twisted, as if he were tasting something bitter, and that moment she knew he believed she had been lying awake, mourning the loss of Judson. If only he knew the real reason she had tossed and turned. . . .

She stiffened and forced herself to walk forward, wishing for once that she were less perceptive. Her hand shook as she poured his coffee. Only her pride and Jamie's presence got her through breakfast. Jamie was her buffer against Jord's sardonic eyes. Her mother had come home even later than Jord and was still in bed.

The day promised to be just as scorching as the rest of the week had been. The sun threw yellow light across the interlocking tile squares of rust and brown on the kitchen floor, leaving no doubt that even at seven o'clock in the morning there was very little coolness in the air.

"I'll finish the barn this morning."

"Are you going to do some more after that?" Jamie asked, laying down the slice of toast he had been munching.

"Yes," Jord said softly, the sound of his voice speaking so gently to Jamie driving pain into Trisha's heart. "I still have the machine shed to finish."

139

"I—I don't have the cash on hand to pay you until after I sell the corn crop," she said. "I'll send the money to your office in the fall."

"I don't want your money." Jord slid to the end of the bench and stood up. "Don't bother to mail it to me anyway," he said, reading her thoughts. "I'll just send it back."

"I wouldn't have allowed you to do the painting if I'd thought you weren't going to accept payment."

He paused. So softly that Jamie couldn't hear he said, "You made your payment last night," and at the stricken look on her face his mouth twisted. He turned his back and walked away.

140

CHAPTER SEVEN

Jamie jumped up and down, his tousled pale gold hair almost touching the canopy of green, blue, and yellow streamers that Trisha had fastened to the dining room ceiling. "Lower, lower," he shouted to the blindfolded Jord, whose hand held the pin that hovered over the expertly drawn picture of the donkey mounted on the wall. "No, no. Higher, higher." Jord's hand moved to the vicinity of the donkey's ear, and Jamie giggled, his feet shifting under him in an excited little dance. His excitement was echoed in the faces of the three small children who watched—and, to a lesser degree, the circle of adults who stood behind them.

The table had been moved out of the way, set back against the wall with its precious load of presents and decorated cake.

Trisha glanced up. Judson, across the room from her, stood with his hands in his pockets, his easy smile a poor attempt to disguise the explosion of joy and pride she knew he must be feeling. Margie caught their shared look and reached out to touch her husband's sleeve, tears of joy in her eyes. She had easily accepted Judson's offhand explanation that both Trisha and Jord felt the time had come to give Jamie the security of living with two loving people who wanted to adopt him very badly. Margie didn't ask the whys and wherefores. She was too happy to do that. She had simply cried a little, hugged Trisha, and agreed that nothing should be said to Jamie until after the party. Judson would have to tell her the truth eventually, of course, but Trisha knew that when he did, Margie would somehow find a way to accept it—and forgive.

Judson tore his eyes away from Jamie and returned her pensive look. As if he remembered that he was taking Jamie away from her, his eyes darkened. She shook her head, a warning gesture that carried her determination not to let anyone guess how her heart was being shredded into bits. Just as she did, Jamie cried, "There, that's it," and collapsed in a fit of giggles as Jord punched the tack into the board, pulled off his blindfold, and turned and looked directly into Trisha's eyes. His gaze whipped across the room, found the object of hers, and darkened with black anger.

"Look, look," Jamie cried, gasping with laughter. Jord, after what seemed like an icy eternity, turned his eyes away from her to look toward the board. The braided tail dangled down directly from the donkey's brown and belligerent eye.

"Why, you little devil," Jord growled with pretended fury, spinning out the fantasy that he had not known Jamie was fooling him, "you tricked me." His anger of a moment ago might never have been.

"I told you wrong, I told you wrong," Jamie chanted triumphantly, dancing up and down on each word. "I told you wrong, and you did it."

"Next time I'll know better than to trust you, you little traitor," he warned in a mock-gruff voice.

It was Mandy's turn at the donkey. She was a charming little cherub with great blue eyes and coffee-brown hair who had won Jamie's heart the first day he'd seen her in his nursery school class. He handed her the tail, and all his desire to tease vanished. "Here, Mandy," he said in a sober, grown-up tone.

The little girl accepted the pin with a grave air and turned her back to Jord, who bent down and fixed Trisha's red scarf over her eyes.

"There, now," he said after he had tied the knot at the back of her head. "Is that too tight?" His gentle fingers, checking the position of the scarf against the girl's dark hair, brought a lump to Trisha's throat.

Mandy shook her head solemnly. No longer able to see, she seemed unable to speak as well.

"You can't see, can you?" Jord asked, and then added teasingly, "I wouldn't want you to have an advantage over me."

Another slow shake of the small head told him she couldn't see.

Jamie whispered solicitously into her ear, "Don't worry, Mandy. I'll help you."

The adults watched with amusement as Jamie turned her around three times and then guided her to the wall. With vocal directions he proceeded to tell her exactly where the tail should go.

Silently Mandy's hand followed his instructions and placed the tail just a little above the proper spot. With great applause she was declared the winner and handed the prize, a small bottle of bubble-blowing fluid with a red plastic wand.

A game of musical chairs followed. Trisha manned the record player and stopped the music in all the unexpected places. Jamie won—with a little conspicuous assistance from his grandmother.

When it was time to cut the cake, the table was moved back into the middle of the room, the chairs were placed around it, and eight places were quickly set with blue paper plates and the green plastic forks and spoons that Jamie had chosen in the store the day before.

Margie lit the candles on the cake, and their glowing reflection burned in Jamie's eyes. "Make a wish," Margie instructed him, and Jamie squeezed his eyes tight, was silent for a moment, then opened them, aimed carefully, and blew out the five candles in one enthusiastic puff.

The cake was chocolate, Jamie's favorite flavor. Margie had begged Trisha to let her bake and decorate it, and Margie had been lavish, making it a three-tiered affair with a cowboy figure perched on his horse sitting at the top. Trisha watched Margie cutting the cake and tried not to think how symbolic its independent little horseman was. Jamie had reached school age and would not only be spending a part of his day away from home but be coming home to Margie and Judson instead of her. How empty her life would be!

To cover her distress, she got up from her chair and hurried out to the kitchen to dish out the ice cream. She was in control by the time she returned with the heavy tray. Even Misty was allowed a share; she sat on the floor licking the creamy treat from her bowl, her pink tongue going in and out of her mouth with slow and deliberate enjoyment.

Jamie opened his presents. He took his time with each one, expressing his pleasure and thanks in a mature way, looking at each giver. He was, in fact, so polished and sure of himself that when he was finished, and the pile of gaily decorated papers from his presents was piled on the floor around him, Judson said softly, "You did that very well—son."

Jamie looked at him. "That's because Aunt Trisha taught me."

"Taught you?" Judson was amused.

Jamie nodded. "Aunt Trisha says it's just as important to learn to receive gifts as it is to give them. She teaches me lots of things, my numbers and letters and stuff."

Judson said thoughtfully, "I see." His eyes swept briefly over Trisha and back to Jamie. "Your Aunt Trisha is a smart lady."

"Yes," Jamie agreed casually, as if it were so obvious he didn't understand why anyone even needed to say it. Losing interest in the whole conversation, he turned to Mandy. "You want to go outdoors and play? We can take Misty."

The little girl found her voice. "Are Terry and Joey coming?"

"Sure, if they want to," Jamie said indifferently. The children trooped away. Trisha rose to clean up, and against her will her eyes connected with Jord's. Hard, sardonic disdain glittered in their depths, and she knew at once why. A casual word of praise from her brother-in-law was all it took to make Jord look at her as if she were beneath his contempt.

That night Jamie was still keyed up. Trisha bathed him, hoping the warm water would help soothe his overstimulated nerves. She wasn't sure it did, but she put him into his Big Bird pajamas, tucked him in bed, and leaned forward to kiss his soap-fragrant cheek.

"I don't feel anything," he said, raising dark eyes to her. "How come I can't feel it if I'm really older?"

"Don't worry," she said, ruffling his wiry blond hair. "Someday you'll feel it and wish you couldn't."

The next morning he was restless, let down. Trisha noticed it immediately at the breakfast table. Even Jord's presence wasn't enough to distract him. He brought the small toy tractor that Mandy had given him to the table, something he knew was expressly forbidden, and ran it along the edge, a *put-putting* sound bubbling from his lips.

"Jamie," Trisha said, controlling her impatience, "put your tractor down on the seat and eat your cereal."

He shook his head, a stubborn little pout pursing his mouth. "I'm not hungry." The *put-putting* sound began again, and the tractor charged the cereal bowl. The bowl caught on the side of the spoon and tilted, spilling milk and cornflakes to the floor.

Trisha said sharply, "Jamie!"

"I'm sorry."

With a feverish haste he raced to the towel bar and grabbed a towel from the rack. He crawled under the table on his hands and knees and with several inexpert swipes cleaned the spilt milk. He handed Trisha the towel, cornflakes clinging to it. His face was at once apprehensive and repentant.

"Oh, Jamie," she said, melting at the distressed look on his face. Taking the towel from him, she gave the boy a quick hug.

145

Then, aware of Jord's eyes on her, "Why don't you take Misty and go outside and play?"

"Okay," Jamie agreed readily and escaped from the kitchen.

"Trisha." Jord's voice was husky and disturbed, but whatever he was going to say was lost to her, for just then her mother came into the kitchen.

Virginia Adams looked from her daughter to Jord. "What on earth is going on out here?"

"Jamie spilled his cereal," Trisha explained, using another cloth to wipe up the puddle Jamie had left on the table.

"I thought at the very least it was a herd of elephants tramping through." Her mother sank onto one of the bench seats in the eating nook.

"I'm sorry," Trisha apologized. "Did we wake you?"

"No, not really," her mother admitted. "I was just lying there, thinking I should get up soon anyway."

There was a silence in the room, and Trisha could feel Jord's eyes on her. Whatever he had been going to say, it couldn't have been anything she wanted to hear. "I've got to get that bean field finished. Will you watch Jamie for me?"

"Yes, of course," her mother said, getting up to go to the stove to get herself a cup of coffee.

"And I've got to finish painting," Jord said. "The sooner the better."

The blood drained away from Trisha's face. Jord didn't see her reaction, for he had gotten quickly to his feet and followed Jamie out without looking back. *It's a good thing. One look at my face would give it all away.*

The bean field, if anything, was hotter than it had been the morning before. She walked several rounds, whacking and chopping at the weeds, venting her anger and frustration on them. *That's for you, Jord Deverone.* A corn plant fell. *And that, and that, and that.*

On the last *that* the handle of the hoe broke, the wood splitting into jagged slivers from just above the iron sleeve to halfway up the wooden dowel. There was no way she could use that hoe now. She would have to walk back to the machine shed and find another.

She cursed softly under her breath, even though there was no one to hear. It was a habit she had gotten into out of consideration for Jamie's tender years and ears.

She was, of course, at the far end of the field. That meant she had to walk all the way back across the hot, plowed ground with a useless hoe in her hand, dig through the assorted old tools in the machine shed in the hope that she could find another, and if she couldn't, take a precious hour and a half of her time driving to Emmetsburg just to buy a new one.

She was not in the best of moods when she walked into the yard, and her disposition did not improve when her mother stepped out of the house and shouted her name.

She trudged closer, leaned her arms on the gate. "What is it?"

Her mother's face looked gray. "I can't find Jamie. He went with me down to water the chickens, but he wandered away, and when I called—he didn't answer."

Trisha's slender body straightened. "How long ago was that?"

"About ten minutes." Virginia Adams took a step forward and gripped the gate as if she needed the support. "I came back to the house to make sure he wasn't here. I was just on my way out to tell Jord when I saw you."

"Did you look in the barn?"

"No, but he would have heard me calling from there, surely. He's never been the type to play tricks—"

"He's not playing tricks. He knows better than that."

She whirled away and ran toward the barn, her weariness forgotten. Once before Misty had gotten away from him and gone into the barn, and perhaps that had happened again. She raced across the grass, praying she was wrong.

Disturbed to find its hook dangling, she jerked open the bottom half of the barn door. "Jamie!"

147

She listened. There was silence and then a muffled sound, like a squeak stifled, or a small boy speaking with a hand over his mouth. She called his name again, the edges of panic creeping into her voice. "Jamie!"

She fought to control her rasping breath in order to hear. She did hear it then, the faintest cry. "I'm here."

Her heart plummeted. His voice was coming from the haymow, the place he had been specifically instructed to stay away from until someone came and stacked the bales.

"Jamie! Where are you!"

The sound came again, a frightened squeak. "Up here, Aunt Trisha."

She went out of the stable part of the barn and pulled open the full door that led directly into the haymow. A makeshift ladder was fastened to the partition of Prince's stall. He whickered at her as she grasped the sides of the ladder, but she ignored him and hauled herself upward. There was a flat platform over the stalls that served as a roof to keep the hay from falling down on Prince's head and was also a storage place of sorts where she could stand up and survey the barn. That was her destination. Once she was up there, she would be able to see the entire haymow.

The ladder seemed endless, even though its top wasn't more than ten feet off the ground. Perspiration crawled down her back, her breathing rasped in her throat. Where was he? Caught under several heavy bales, the life slowly leaving him?

She gained the top and swung over the side. She straightened on the stall roof and scanned the bales. They were lying at crazy angles on top of one another, just as she knew they would be, like dominoes a child had thrown down. And at the peak of the pile, on a bale that looked as unstable as a rock on the point of a mountain, sat Jamie. Misty mewed and struggled in his hands.

"My God!" she breathed. Then louder, to Jamie, "Don't move."

"I'm not," Jamie squeaked. "I'm not even talking loud. I

couldn't talk loud enough for Grandma to hear me. I was afraid everything would fall down."

Trisha made an effort to grab back the terror that crawled along her nerves like fire. "You did exactly the right thing, honey. Don't move. I'll just have to think a minute"—this was an understatement—"about how I'm going to get you out of there."

Nervously Jamie did exactly what she had told him not to do and shifted his legs. The bale not immediately under him but the next one down teetered ominously. A short, vivid word escaped her lips.

"What the hell is going on?" At the sound of Jord's voice she felt overwhelming relief. She glanced down, saw the top of his head, the gold of his hair dimmed in the faint light. The sight of him had never been more welcome. "Jord. Up here."

He looked up and saw her. "It's Jamie," she said quietly, not wanting to alarm either of them. "Take the ladder."

When Jord had swung easily up beside her, she said to him under her breath, "Look."

He muttered a succinct word that was a favorite of his. "How the hell did he manage that?"

"I haven't asked. Chasing the cat, I suppose."

Jord swore again. "His weight didn't disturb that mess, but mine sure as hell will."

"Jord." She caught his arm. "Maybe Jamie can crawl out the way he came in."

"Does he look like he can?" Jord nodded toward the boy, who was so white he looked almost ghostly in the dim light. "Just let me look at the pile a minute. Maybe I can find some stability in this mess if I study it."

He stood stock still, scanning the bales.

"Can you get me out of here?" Jamie asked him tearfully.

"You bet I will," Jord assured him. "You just sit tight so you're still there when I come for you."

149

He studied for a moment longer and then turned to Trisha. "If anything goes wrong, don't come in after us. Go get help."

"Jord—"

"Promise me," he grated.

"No," she said, shaking her head. "How could I leave—"

He reached out and caught her arm. "Promise, damn you."

She stared up at him, her cheeks burning, her mouth defiant. Her hand hidden against her thigh, she crossed one finger over the other. "If that's what you want."

He relaxed slightly and let her go. "Go over and stand there, just opposite where he is. Just to be on the safe side, as soon as I can, I'll hand him to you."

"Jord—be careful."

He gave her a dark, engimatic look, and then the mocking smile lifted his lips. "I hadn't exactly planned on being careless."

He stepped off the flat, safe surface of the constructed ceiling onto the first bale. It wobbled slightly—and held. He stepped to another, and another. The third teetered crazily, bringing her heart to her throat. Jord performed a balancing act, stretching his arms out and sliding his feet to a more stable position. One more step would bring him next to Jamie. He tried the bale in front of him. It held for a moment, but as he went to shift his weight it gave suddenly and tumbled end over end to land with a crash on the cement floor that had been the dairy part of the barn in the days when Trisha's father had milked cows. Like a sensitive volcano, the rest of the pile shook, but the part that supported Jamie and Jord held.

Trisha's heart climbed crazily to the base of her throat and stayed there, beating at a frantic rate. "Jord—"

"Shh—it's all right.

"I'm scared," Jamie whimpered, and Jord's voice said softly, "Only a fool wouldn't be, son. Just hang on for a few more seconds. I'm almost there."

But he wasn't almost there. The bale that fell had been an important link, and now Jord was forced to approach Jamie by a more circuitous route. He stepped sideways to one bale—and another—and another, placing his feet as gingerly as if the bales were shifting ice floes.

When he was just within reaching distance, he warned Jamie softly, "Don't move, son. Let me reach for you."

Jord leaned forward and collected Jamie off the bale. Jamie, for all his self-control, fairly leaped into Jord's arms, and the slight kick his feet gave the bale that had been his resting place sent it tumbling off the stack toward the south end of the barn. Almost running, Jord crossed the short distance to Trisha and reached out with his precious package. She grabbed Jamie, pulling his warm body close with a sense of relief—only to turn and see the hay bale Jord had used for balance collapse like a broken board. Jord fought valiantly to stay on his feet, but he couldn't. He went tumbling down into the center of the pile, with the bales that formed the under part of Jamie's perch following him.

She stared down at him in horror. Dust and hay leaves rose and filled her nostrils, choking her.

"Jord!" Her voice rose shrilly.

"I'm all right," he groaned. "I just can't—breathe. Too damn —dusty."

"Jamie. Go get Grandma. Tell her to get help. Go! Go!"

He thumped across the echoing wood floor and scrabbled down the ladder, holding Misty. When she saw that he was out of the barn safely, she turned back to Jord. Four bales lay on top of his legs in a drunken sort of pyramid, but, thank God, his chest and face were free.

She took a breath, and in the quiet of the barn Jord heard it.

"Don't do anything foolish," he said through gritted teeth. "Stay away from me. You promised."

"I had my fingers crossed," she said and stepped off the platform to walk across the bales toward him.

Jord roused up, the effort making him gasp in pain. "Goddammit, woman, stay away!"

She ignored him. Her mind was working at top speed, and

with a superhuman strength she pushed the top two bales to one side, away from Jord. The third was wedged against another one, and she had to give it a mighty heave to send it in the direction she wanted it to go, away from Jord's head.

"The Incredible Hulk," he murmured, and she coughed and sneezed, the dust and leaves swirling around both of them.

She took hold of the last, most difficult bale to move. It was lodged between two others. Jord coughed, a choking, gasping cough, and in desperation she pulled the twine around the corner of the packed hay, and the bale broke and showered Jord with more hay and dust, covering his face. She screamed "No!" and dropped to her knees and began to claw away the hay, until his beloved face appeared among the gray-green sticks and leaves. "Oh, thank God," she gasped.

"Your rescue technique leaves something to be desired," he growled with sardonic amusement, bending and pushing himself upright, doing his best to get to his feet on the unsteady surface of the bale beneath him. "You could have suffocated me."

"I'm sorry," she said between coughs. "Are you all right? Is anything broken?"

"I don't think so," he said, making testing movements of his arms and legs. "I just can't breathe, that's all. Let's get out of here."

He held her arm, and together, supporting each other, they crawled over the now more stable pile toward the door.

Outside she said to him anxiously, "Are you sure you're all right?"

He looked down at her, amusement and something that, had he been looking at anyone else, she might have interpreted as admiration in his eyes.

"Well, let's see. I had four forty-pound bales on me—that's roughly equivalent to the weight and size of one of the women Rubens used for models." He squinted down at Trisha. "I think I'll live."

Her voice crisp, she said, "I'm sure you will."

"I'd better finish my painting."

"No," she said. "Go up to the house and have a shower and take a rest."

He shook his head. "I don't think so. I want to get this done."

"You're leaving."

"Yes."

She stifled the urge to reach up and brush the dry hay leaves out of his hair and twisted away from him to look at the house that was set in the grove, the grove that she would never again look at without thinking of Jord. She thrust her hands into the pockets of her jeans and fought back the tears. A dry hay leaf that had dropped in that unlikely place crumpled at the touch of her fingers. "Don't—don't forget to tell Jamie good-bye."

"I won't," he said softly.

Her mother gave the emergency ambulance crew, a man-and-wife team, glasses of iced tea and some of her gingersnap cookies. They were gracious about the misunderstanding and said they'd far rather be called and not needed than needed and not called. Jamie was properly chastised and didn't venture outside the yard during the remainder of the afternoon.

Trisha spent the rest of the day trudging up and down the bean field, the empty, dead feeling inside her growing with every step she took.

During supper Jord avoided her eyes. She thought she hid her distress rather well, but when he was finished eating and asked for permission to ride Prince, she was forced to look at him and nod. Their eyes met, and the silence seemed to drum in her ears. Whatever he was thinking, he didn't want her to guess, for he quickly shut her out by dropping those heavily lashed lids.

He slid out of the eating nook and left the house. Shamelessly she went to the window and watched until he came out of the barn with Prince, swung up into the saddle, and rode out of the yard. He crested the hill, and his head slowly disappeared as he went down the other side. She turned away from the window. Her mother said nothing, but her eyes were eloquent.

Later Trisha was sitting in the living room, apathetically watching a rerun of a rerun, when her mother offered to put Jamie to bed for her. Trisha accepted the offer. She stayed where she was, one leg flung over the chair. She told herself it was walking through the bean field that had made her too tired to move, but she knew that wasn't true. The television program changed to a documentary she just wasn't interested in, and she was ready to give it up and go upstairs to bed when her mother returned to the living room. "Hasn't Jord been gone for quite a while?"

At the sound of his name Trisha roused from her lazy position in the chair. "I don't know. Has he?"

"It's been almost an hour and a half. That's a long time for a man who's not used to riding to be out on a horse. It's nearly dark."

Trisha felt the first little tingle of alarm. Suppose he had been more badly hurt than anyone realized? Suppose he was suffering from the aftereffects of concussion or—Prince had thrown him?

She swung her leg over the chair arm and scrambled to her feet. "I'll go look for him. He can't have gone too far."

"You do that, dear," her mother said, her voice bland. "Otherwise we'll both sit here and worry."

The pickup was dustier than ever when she climbed inside, and it seemed to rattle her right to the bone as she drove down the lane. At the end of the lane she hesitated. North or south? Going on instinct, she turned north. Perhaps Jord would be drawn toward the lake, just as she was.

She could see nothing from the top of the hill, and even less from the little hollow at the bottom. She turned right onto the main road and drove for the short distance it took to bring her to the old lake road, the one close to the shore, and turned left on it.

The sun was low on the horizon, still sending out gold rays to

154

light the sky. It wouldn't last long, though. She guessed she had a half hour of daylight, perhaps, and about the same amount of twilight, no more. But if he wasn't here, if he was lying somewhere at the side of the road. . . .

Her mind skidded to a halt, refused to go further. He would be all right. He had to be.

She reached the point, the place where, years ago, there had been a pavilion. There were still three picnic tables in rather sad disrepair sitting under the trees, but it was no longer a popular spot because of the lack of a source of drinking water. At one of the trees Prince stood, stretching his neck down to crop the grass. He was securely tethered, his reins tied to a low branch.

Relief simmered through her. She drove the pickup into the approach lane, stopped the engine, pocketed the keys, and got out. She was almost sure she knew where Jord was and what he was doing, but she had to be certain.

She forced herself to saunter casually toward the point. The sandy beach had been a favorite swimming place. And it was here she had first felt the strength of Jord's arms and known the heady feel of his body against hers.

She saw his head moving above the surface of the water. He was swimming in a fast crawl, his elbows bending to slice the water at the exactly the right angle and propel his body forward at a fast rate. His feet made a slight ripple above the surface. He had obviously spent many hours swimming since his summers here. Did he swim at a club in the city? Or did he have an apartment with one of the fabulous rooftop pools she had read about? How little she knew about him.

From somewhere over her head a meadowlark trilled its long, intricate song. Jord stopped swimming and trod water, shaking the hair out of his eyes, twisting his body to look back at the shore. He saw her then, but she was too far away to read his expression. She only knew that he gazed at her for what seemed like endless minutes. Then he ducked his head and began to swim—toward her.

155

She saw it then, the neat little pile of his clothes: shirt, jeans, and dark briefs like the ones she had put in the dryer, folded and piled on top of the caramel-colored leather boots. And while she was looking at his clothes he swam into the shallow water . . . and stood up.

She lifted her eyes. She should have looked away—but she couldn't. The fading light gave him a golden sheen, turned the hair around his head to a darker gold. Slick wet body, lean flanks, and flat stomach, light golden-brown hair covering his chest, darker whorls on his thighs and legs. A man. The man she loved.

He walked steadily, inexorably toward her. Her own bone and muscle seemed to have turned to water. Legs, ankles, knees, nothing worked. The connection between brain and nerve endings was broken. Yet, strangely, she seemed more alive than she had ever been in her life. She heard the sand crunch under his feet as he left the water, saw the tiny droplets caught in his chest hairs, heard the slightly accelerated sound of his breathing.

At the edge of the water he stopped. "What are you doing here?"

He was totally at ease, not a self-conscious inch to his body. And she could see every inch of him. She tried to match his dispassionate tone. "Looking for you."

"Well, you've found me."

"Yes," she breathed, giving him a long, slow, up-and-down look. "Haven't I."

Her fervent tone made him laugh. "I think," he said evenly, "you'd better go—before I have to get back into that water to cool off again."

"I'm the one who—needs to cool off."

He stood, not a muscle in his body moving—waiting. It was as if the night on the schoolhouse lawn had never happened. He seemed to have left his cold, contemptuous voice and face somewhere in the lake behind him. She hoped he never found it again.

His eyes were warm with desire, and she knew hers must be glowing with the same heated need.

She made no move toward him, waiting for him to make some sign that he wanted her with him. There was a long, endless silence. Even the bird had stopped singing. Then, slowly, as if he were forcing his muscles to obey his will, he turned to walk back into the water.

She almost cried out in despair. She had made a mistake. She had been waiting—and he had been waiting. Neither of them had wanted to make the first move, to betray the need. And tomorrow he would be gone—and there would be no reason for him ever to return.

"Jord."

Her pulses raged wildly along her veins. Was he going to keep his back turned to her forever?

At knee depth he twisted around, met her eyes. "Yes?"

"May I—join you?"

He gazed at her for another long beat of time. The blood pounded in her ears. "Did you bring your swimsuit?" His tone was smooth, noncommittal.

Was he going to refuse her on that flimsy pretext? The blood rushed to her cheeks. He didn't want her. "No."

"In that case"—he grinned, a boyish grin she had never seen before—"I'd be delighted to have you join me."

Relief and surprise surged through her. She kicked off her sandals and reached for the bottom of her T-shirt. The movement of her hand was the impetus that stung him into action. He turned his back to her and ran into the water, ducking his head to surface dive and submerge his body.

She knew why he had left her. She had felt it, too, that sensual excitement that reached out and grabbed her throat and made her desperately want to run into his arms and feel his wet, naked body pressed against hers. . . . The T-shirt came off easily, but her fingers fumbled with the snap of her bra, the zipper of her jeans. When the last article of her clothing, bikini panties with tiny blue polka dots, was placed on the pile, she faced the water. He was out just far enough to stand submerged—and he was watching her. She should have been shivering in the night air—but she wasn't. She felt warm to the very core.

The water wasn't icy, but it wasn't bath-water warm, either. After she moved around a bit, she felt better. The lake was spring-fed, and there were cold spots where the springs bubbled up and warm spots where the sun had shone, and when she got used to a sudden change in temperature every so often, she felt the silky water slide over her skin and reveled in the sensual pleasure it gave her.

The lake had a very gradual slope. She tilted her legs down and found she was where she could stand and keep her head out. She straightened and flipped her hair out of her eyes. She was sleeking it back over her head and looking around for Jord when two hands caught her at the waist and pulled her back against a muscular chest.

"Lorelei," he murmured in her ear, his lips finding her temple. "Did she have black hair?"

"Probably not." She put her hands on top of his, struggling to maintain a hold on her reeling senses. "And she couldn't have been as tall as I am—"

He turned her in his arms and stopped her self-deprecatory words with a hard kiss, his mouth cool and wet on hers. It was a chastising kiss, swift and sweet.

He raised his mouth. "You're exactly right," he murmured against her lips. "Feel how you fit against my body. Perfect."

She felt the way her hips curved into his, the long bare length of his thighs pressed against hers . . . and the evidence of his desire . . . "Jord, I—"

He tightened his grip on her waist. "Don't lose your courage now." His voice was low, husky. His hands traveled the length of her spine, found the lovely erotic spot at its base. "Stay with me. I won't do anything you don't want me to do."

CHAPTER EIGHT

"I'm not afraid of you," she said in a blinding blaze of truth. "I'm afraid of myself, afraid of losing control, afraid of frightening you—"

He was nonplussed. The caressing hands stilled. He drew back in amazement and stared down into her face. "Are you serious?"

She hesitated and then said, "Yes."

He stared down at her as if assessing the truth of her words. Then he smiled a dark, wicked smile. "Are you bragging—or complaining?"

Because she had burned all her bridges and crossed the Rubicon the moment she stepped into the water, she said in a low, choked tone, "Please—don't laugh. You've—been a fantasy of mine for a long time."

She waited, breath held, her eyes riveted on his face. Very few men could have handled the twofold blast of honesty she had handed him. If he still believed she loved Judson, and wanted to back out, let him do it now. But at least she had made it clear that for her this was no casual encounter.

He gazed down at her. "How long have you had this—fantasy?"

159

She tilted her head. It took every ounce of courage she had, but she met his eyes. "Since the first time I saw you. I was seven years old, I think."

He considered that for a moment, watching her, as if he didn't believe her. If he wanted to withdraw, she had given him an out. He could brush her aside and say he wasn't interested in being any woman's fantasy, let alone hers. His slow drawl penetrated her dismal thoughts. "Now you *are* frightening me." That amused smile tilted the corners of his mouth. "I'm not sure I can live up to a fantasy *that* old." He gave her a bland, stand-up-comic, I've-just-delivered-my-line look.

She laughed, her amusement heightened by tension and desire. "Why, you—" She wrapped her arms around his neck and tried to shove him beneath the surface of the water, but he was too tightly entwined with her. He tightened his grip, wrapped his legs around hers to throw her off balance. They went down together.

In her wild attempts to free herself from Jord's hands and legs, she knocked her elbow against the bottom. There was an instant pain as skin scraped against sand.

In the thrash of legs and arms and bodies Jord was unaware of her injury. Satisfied that she had been properly subdued, he readjusted his hold to lift her out of the water. She sputtered and coughed.

"Leg wrestling is against ground rules," she told him, pushing her hair back out of her eyes, very aware of his hands locked around her waist, his palms pressed against the small of her back as they stood together in the water.

"Whose ground rules?"

"The ones I just made up."

He bent his head and brushed his mouth along her wet cheek, his tongue licking away a drop of water. "Who's going to follow ground rules made up by the woman who crosses her fingers when she makes promises?"

"Jord—I couldn't just stand there and let you suffocate—or worse."

He kissed her cheek, her temple, the tender spot just in front of her ear. "Fantasies aren't allowed to suffocate, is that it?"

Now she was the one who felt the need to lighten the mood with humor. "Certainly not. Not in dusty old haymows, anyway. At the very least a dark Gothic house with a winding stair— Jord, please—"

He had pushed her hair away and was exploring the shell of her ear with his tongue. "Any self-respecting fantasy starts with a woman's ear."

But he was no longer a fantasy. He was solid flesh and muscle and bone, and it suddenly occurred to her that he had given her his tacit permission to indulge her dreams with him in any way she cared to.

"Jord."

He lifted his head. The sun was nearly gone, but in the twilight she saw the blaze of hunger in his eyes.

He made no move toward her. He merely waited with those glowing eyes.

She caught his face between her hands, and slowly, carefully feathered light, loving kisses over his face, on his cheeks, his eyes. His wet lashes were tantalizing her mouth with their tickling softness. She kissed the place where his hair grew back from his temple, and the tip of his nose. Her hands moved around to the back of his head, found the silky wetness of his nape hair, and stroked it while her mouth sought his lips, touching their full sensual lines with teasing off-and-on caresses.

She could feel him fighting to hold his body still, to play out his role of recipient, to let her continue to bathe his face with kisses. But when her mouth slipped lower, to the hollow of his throat, and lower still to the sensitive male nipple, he stifled a word and bent his head to capture her mouth with his.

His lips were warm and possessive on hers. His tongue probed gently at first, and then more insistently, until her mouth throbbed with warmth and fullness. Her body felt every inch of him pressed against her, his chest against her breasts, his hips molded to hers, his thighs hard and supporting her own.

Then his hand traveled down, over her breast, and came up from underneath the full curve to find and tease the already taut peak to an even fuller crest. His caress was expert, arousing. Delight tingled from the pit of her abdomen up through her, making her gasp with its strength.

He leaned forward to taste the essence of that sensitive bud, and then slowly, sensually, just as he had that day in the bean field, he stroked her nipple with his tongue, cleansing the water away. She took another sharp breath and clutched his back.

"Now," he said, raising his head to look at her, his voice low and amused, "we both need to be cooled off."

She should have been warned by that tone of amused mischief, but she was still grappling with her reaction to his mouth at her breast. He released her, walked away a step, and stretched his hand down into the water. He brought it up, his cupped hand splashing her shoulders, her breasts, her midriff. The water stung her into life, shocked her system. A moment ago she had been held next to his very warm, very male body. Now she was being pelted with water that felt far colder than it really was.

She came after him, determined to give him as good as he gave, but he churned through the water toward the beach, luring her to the shallow edge. When he was in water just to his ankles, he gave up the chase so abruptly she skidded into his back. He turned and pulled her into his arms.

"I think you caught me," he murmured into her hair.

"I think I have."

"What's my punishment?"

She tilted her head, as if giving his question her entire consideration when in actuality she could hardly think at all with every solid inch of his naked body pressing against hers without the surrounding silkiness of the water. Then, provocatively, she smiled. "I'll think of something."

His hands moved over her back, traced the roundness of her hips and the curve lower down. "I was hoping you would."

She stood in his arms and laid her head against his shoulder, thinking this must surely be paradise, this little shaded cove on a deserted lake. The light was nearly gone. A rosy glow lit the sky and turned the water to the same hue. The crickets chirped softly in the grass, and the water lapped with a self-satisfied sound against the shore.

"We do have this problem—" he said slowly.

She raised her head. "Which is?"

"We need something to lie on," he said softly.

"I keep a sleeping bag in the pickup tucked behind the seat."

He raised a dark eyebrow. "Do you?" he drawled, the words suggestive, questioning.

She bit his chin lightly in mock punishment. "It's there to wrap up Jamie in the wintertime. The pickup heater doesn't work too well."

"That's a relief." He wrapped a long, wet silky strand of her hair around his wrist and used it to bring her lips close to his.

"Jord, about Judson—"

"Shh." He put his mouth over hers, as if he were enthralled with the texture and curve it.

"You know—the truth?"

"Let's say that I—guessed."

"When? How?"

He smiled down at her, and there in that dark and private twilight she thought it was without a doubt the most beautiful smile she had ever seen in the whole of her life.

"If you could have seen your face when you were digging me out of the hay." He leaned forward and brushed her nose with his mouth. "You have a very beautiful, expressive face, my love. And it told me something I'd been too blind to see before."

She felt almost light-headed with relief. He knew she loved him. And he wasn't embarrassed or distressed or displeased. But then, he had never made a secret of his desire for her. He wanted to make love to her—but he didn't love her.

As if he had read her mind, he murmured in her ear, "About that sleeping bag—"

She braced her arms and pushed at him. "I'll go get it."

"No. I'll go. You stay here."

He walked away over the cool grass, his lithe stride seemingly unhindered by the fact he had nothing on his feet.

She spread out her jeans and sat down on them and tucked her legs up to her chin for warmth. The breeze hit her damp skin, and suddenly the night was chill, and her thoughts cooled along with the air. She loved him, true. But he didn't love her. To him she would be just a woman he'd met in the country, a pleasant change—but hardly someone he could spend the rest of his life with. She simply wasn't his kind of woman.

She was shivering when he returned. He unrolled the bag and ran the zipper round it. "Come on, honey, get in. You look like you're freezing. I shouldn't have splashed you just as we were getting out, but you deserved it. That mouth of yours should be registered."

"Jord, I—"

He stared down at her. "You are cold, aren't you? Right down to your feet, you little coward." He leaned over her, and his voice was hard. He pulled her off the ground and hauled her to her feet, brought her up against the hard, lean length of his body. He held her there, and even in the dark she could see the fury in his eyes. "Let me tell you something, Miss Flannery. I'm far too old to be led on with a few teasing kisses and then told to be a good boy and go away. If you think you're going to play that game with me, you can think again." His mouth came down on hers ruthlessly, his tongue plundering her mouth, probing, taunting. His hands gripped the soft flesh of her upper arms. He locked her to him at breast and hip and thigh.

For a moment she was stunned and went weak like a helpless doll under the onslaught of his rough kiss. But then everything

164

changed. His fury acted as a trigger, dispelling all the doubts—and releasing the pent-up passion she had been harboring for years. She met his kiss with a wild fury of her own. Her tongue answered his touch for touch, and her body melted into the contours of his with fluid feminine grace. If he was hungry for her, she was starving for him.

Her response seemed to dissolve his anger. "Trisha, my God, don't do this to me. I won't force you, you know that, but if you want me to stop, get away from me now."

She tightened her hold, digging her fingers into his back. "I don't want you to stop," she whispered. "I want you to love me. . . ."

Together they knelt and stretched out on the downy softness of the sleeping bag. He saw to her comfort, pulling the heavy duck material around her. Then he lay down beside her and pulled her into his arms, and the wonderful, agonizing heaven began all over again. He warmed her body with his hands and his lips, murmuring soft love words to her as his hands pleasured her. He kissed her shoulders, the soft skin between her breasts, rediscovered with his mouth and tongue and lips their passion-darkened centers. His hands wandered over her abdomen, and down the smooth curve of her thighs to linger again at the sweet and secret femininity of her. She moaned and writhed under his touch, knowing that this time there was no going back, that the hand that touched her was trembling with a passion that matched her own. Her fingers sought and found his back, cool and silky from his swim. She smoothed her palms over that satiny skin, knowing that if she could have absorbed him through the pads of her fingers, she would have. She wanted to merge with him, to blend her body with his. She continued to touch him, to let her hands come around to his chest. Her fingers found the sensitive places on his chest, the round nubs that responded to her touch. She leaned forward and teased one with her tongue, her hands wandering lower, bestowing on him the same sweet pleasure he was giving her.

"Trisha." Her name came out in a hoarse, uncontrolled sound. He buried his mouth in the soft pulse spot of her throat, as if he, too, wanted to consume her. Gently his thigh nudged against hers, and his heavy weight moved over her. He was trembling. "I'm afraid I'll hurt you. The ground is hard—"

He was heavy—but his chest crushing her breasts, his body pressed against hers was an erotic delight. "I'm all right."

"Are you sure?"

"Jord, I want you. I—"

He answered her unspoken plea and there, in the night and the darkness, they became one. She knew then what it meant to be a woman, what she had been born for. She had been born to know Jord's body, to be a part of his flesh and his blood and his soul, to build with him the titanic feeling of growing and growing and growing until they both exploded into a fiery nova of light and heat and love. . . .

In the sweet, indolent aftermath he lay beside her, his hand cupping her breast. She shivered, and he leaned over her and kissed her on the mouth. His hand trailed down the length of her bare body. "Time for you to go home, Lady Godiva."

"My hair's not long enough."

He tugged at a long silky length of it and drapped it over one breast. "You're right, it isn't, you indecent woman. Then what are you doing out on a night like this?"

"I was looking for a man—"

He chuckled, let his hand fall away. "Did you find him?"

"Yes," she breathed, reaching out and touching his mouth with her fingertips, "I did." He was still for a moment, obviously savoring the sensual enjoyment of her fingers on his mouth.

Gently he grasped her fingers and tugged them away from his lips. She felt him moving beside her, getting to his feet. "Well, since neither of us has the right length hair, we'll have to be much more prosaic and get dressed, I'm afraid."

Even in the darkness she could see the smooth tan on his skin

166

as he turned his back to her and went with very little stumbling directly to the pile of his clothes. She turned on her side and propped her head on her elbow, watching him dress—as well as she could in the dark. He was nothing but a dark form that moved and bent occasionally.

Fully dressed, he leaned down and kissed her again. "Get your clothes on before you catch your death."

"It's warm," she said lazily, wishing she had the nerve to reach up and unbutton his shirt and pull him down to her again. . . .

"Get up, woman," he said sternly, the amusement lurking just under the gruffness. "Virginia will be worried."

Trisha was jolted out of her languid state. "Good heavens. I'd forgotten. She sent me out for you. She'll probably have the fire department and the sheriff and the emergency ambulance out looking for the pair of us."

"Maybe not."

He turned away and was back in an instant with her clothes in his hand. He stood beside her and stared out over the lake while she pulled on her underthings and struggled into her T-shirt and jeans.

"What do you mean?"

"I mean I think she knows what the circumstances are."

"And what are the circumstances?"

There was a silence, and every second of it made her nerves go taut. "We'll talk about it when we get home." The teasing, the amused indulgence had vanished from his voice. He was utterly serious—and his seriousness sent a little dart of fear through her.

The house was dark. When he had stabled Prince and they had gone inside, they saw that her mother's door was closed. A note lay on the kitchen table. *Trisha: I assumed since I didn't hear any sirens that you found Jord and he was all right. Jamie cried out once in his sleep, but he seems all right now. I was too tired to stay up any longer. I'll see you in the morning. Love, Mother.*

Together they turned off the lights in the house and climbed the stairs. At the top they went into Jamie's room, and as Trisha stood looking down at the sleeping boy she indulged in the most fantastic dream of all, that the tousled blond boy was their child, hers and Jord's. . . .

Even the warmth of his arm around her waist as they walked down the hall together didn't dispell the chill of knowing she would never have Jord's child. But he was still here, beside her, and she would savor every moment of his presence. When he turned her into her bedroom and closed the door behind them, she didn't protest. Instead she whispered, "You said we were going to talk."

He pressed her down gently on the bed and covered her mouth, half-lying on her, slipping his hands under her hips to readjust them to the angle of his own. She was pressed against him, intimately accommodating the hard length of his body with her own soft curves. His tongue explored her moist sweetness, and his hand cupped the provocative curves of her bottom. Now there was a sweet familiarity about his touch and his kiss, and the passion that seemed to have been there, waiting, just under the surface flared again. She reached for him, slipping her hands under his shirt, which was still cool from his ride through the dewy night.

"Now which would you rather do, talk—or this?" He kissed her long and sweetly.

"This," she breathed. "Oh, this."

But afterward, after he had carefully and slowly undressed her and taken that exquisite journey over her with his mouth and hands, and taken her once again to that explosive sensual world where nothing existed for her but Jord and the delight he created, he lay beside her and said, "I must leave in the morning."

"I know."

"I would ask you to come with me, but it isn't possible—you'd need a passport and—"

She stopped listening. She was fighting back the tears, fighting for composure. She hadn't expected him to make it so perfectly clear that she had no part in his life.

"—but I want you to think about it, think about it carefully."

"I—will." What was there to think about?

"That's why I'm leaving without you. I want you to have time to think it over—away from me. I know how much living here means to you. I knew it even before you showed me that damn cornerstone."

Thoroughly arrested now, she lay awake listening as attentively as if her life depended on it. She had the queer feeling that it did. Jord went on in that strange, slightly disturbed tone. "But I'm asking you anyway. If you decide you could leave the country and come and live with me in New York, I'm sure Judson could take over the farm and would welcome the chance to have more land. If you do decide to come to me, I'll expect you to fly out to New York as soon as I come back from Switzerland. I'll call you and—"

"Jord!" She sat up and leaned over him. "You want me to come and—be with you?"

He made an impatient sound. "Haven't you been listening?"

"I thought you were telling me good-bye, so I stopped listening."

He pulled her roughly to him and kissed her with a demanding mouth. "Well, start, will you? I'll be back the eighth of August. Can you remember that? The eighth of August, Trisha. I'll call you that night. I want you by that phone ready to give me your answer."

"But I can give you my answer now—"

He shook his head. "No. I want you to take your time and make your decision after you've thought about it over a period of several days—and with a cool head." He kissed her again long and deeply. When he raised his head, he said, "I want you to be very sure, Trisha."

She was, and she wanted to tell him that, to convince him that she never wanted to be parted from him again. But he was adamant and closed off her protest with a kiss, and then there was no more need for words.

But the next morning, when she stood at the window and watched Jord stride to the gray car dressed in a light-blue suit that transformed him back into the successful urbane businessman he was, a primitive superstition made a chill shiver over her skin. They were light-years apart, she and Jord, and she didn't need to see him dressed in a suit from Savile Row and carrying an attaché case by Pierre Cardin to get the point.

Away from Jord, the slight trickle of insecurity that began when she saw him leave became a roaring river through the broken dam of her self-confidence. She did the normal things, ate breakfast, talked to Jamie and her mother. But her thoughts were devastating. She had given him her heart and soul—and he insisted that she make her decision with a cool head. Was that because he knew exactly how she would react once he was gone? Did he know she would be assailed by doubts, riddled with insecurity? Did he count on her own common sense to do what he didn't have the courage to do, make it clear that she was merely an "evening's entertainment"?

"You found Jord, then," Virginia Adams asked, her eyes keen.

The words jerked her back to the present, but Jord was the last topic she would have chosen for conversation. "Yes, he was swimming."

"I see." Her mother gave her a sharp, knowing look. "I thought that's probably where he was. I'm glad you stayed until he finished having his swim. After all, it's dangerous—swimming alone."

"Yes, that's true. I—waited until he finished, and then we—came home." Which was the truth as far as it went.

"I'm sorry I missed saying good-bye to him this morning."

"He—he said to thank you for your hospitality."

"My hospitality?" Her mother raised a dark eyebrow. "Seems to me he should thank you rather than me. You were with him more than I was."

Trisha shot a look at her, but her mother's face was smooth, unexpressive.

"What are you planning to do today?"

"Rearrange those bales in the barn before somebody else gets hurt," she answered, a touch of grimness around her mouth.

Her mother made a sound of protest. "Why don't you give Judson a call? He would probably come over and do it for you—"

"No." Trisha shook her head. "It's my responsibility. I'll do it."

Her mother frowned. "That sense of responsibility of yours is a little overworked, don't you think? I've often thought so."

Trisha gave her a faint smile. "If it is, I have you to thank for it."

"No, I don't think so. I can blame your father for it; he's not here to defend himself."

Somehow the topic of her father and his sense of responsibility to the land and the farm he had spent his life building up were not things Trisha particularly wanted to think about either. "Mother, I really do have to get to work." She slid out of the breakfast nook and had turned when her mother's voice stopped her.

"Trisha."

She turned. "Yes?"

"Don't let that overworked sense of responsibility think you need to watch out for me. If you want something, reach for it. You have a right to live your own life. Now that Jamie's future has been settled, I—things may change for you. If—if you should decide you want to leave the farm, don't hesitate on my account. I can take care of myself."

171

A world of unspoken love shimmered in her mother's eyes. Impulsively Trisha stepped forward and hugged her.

"Remember that, honey," her mother said, holding her away, looking into her eyes.

"I'll—remember."

She thought of nothing else as she worked in the barn, shifting bales around. She started at the north end of the barn, near the open door, but she was forced to drag out the handkerchief she had stuck in her pocket and tie it over her mouth if she wanted to continue to breathe.

An hour and a half later her arms ached, and she was perspiring heavily. Her old blue blouse, which resembled a man's work shirt, was covered with dust and dry hay leaves, and her jeans were in no better shape. But the bales were in reasonable order, the higher stacks in the back, the lower in the front, and she could walk across them without being thrown off balance. She would use the two bales that had fallen down as feed for Prince. She surveyed her work with a sense of pride. The task had also given her a chance to vent her fears and frustrations, and for the time she had been busy there in the hay, she had simply shut Jord out of her mind. But now that she was finished, he crept in. She thought of the way he had coolly walked across that booby-trapped pile and plucked Jamie from the top of it. . . .

She scrambled down to the floor of the barn and told herself she'd feel better if she had some fresh air. She opened the door— and saw the car at once. For a moment she thought she was crazy, that Jord had returned. But as she began to walk toward the house she saw that the car was a slightly darker gray, even though it was the same general make and model. It was another rental car.

As she approached the sidewalk the door opened. Diane stood there, sleek and soignée in a linen suit of a plum shade that set off the raven glory of her hair, her expertly shaped brows pulled together in impatience. Her eyeshadow matched and enlarged her dark, slightly slanted eyes. Her legs were encased in sheer silk stockings, and her sandals had the look of good, expensive leather.

"Good heavens." As Trisha walked closer Diane wrinkled her nose. "You smell like the barn. What have you been doing?"

"Working," Trisha said shortly. "What have you been doing?"

"Well, actually, flying around the country trying to catch Jord. He asked me to go to Switzerland with him, but Mother tells me I just missed him. Do you know if he was flying out of Kennedy or La Guardia?"

CHAPTER NINE

Trisha stared at her sister from just inside the doorway. Her blood seemed to pause, then race around her body with a new, ferocious rhythm. "No—no I don't. He didn't say."

Diane let the door swing shut behind her and favored her sister with another bored look. No conventional *hello's* or *how are you's* from Diane, Trisha thought warily. This lady was too busy thinking of her own problems.

"What a pain!" Diane continued with her complaints. "Now I'll have to fly over by myself and try to find a room in the same hotel. He's staying on Lake Lucerne, his secretary said."

"Life's little trials," Trisha muttered and walked into the kitchen. Diane trailed after her, the scent of Arpege wafting in her wake. Virginia Adams stood at the sink, but as her daughters came into the room she turned to look at them. A strained expression brought lines to the side of her mouth.

Trisha asked softly, "Where's Jamie?"

"He's playing at Mandy's," her mother answered in an equally low tone. "Margie came and took him over."

In a louder tone, Trisha said, "I've got to get a shower." She gave her sister a sardonic look. "As you said, I smell like the barn."

"I'll come down and talk to you while you get cleaned up," Diane said casually, slipping out of her jacket, the aside about Jamie missing her completely. She wore a silky shell underneath and no bra. Her breasts pressed against the expensive silk.

"I hardly think you're dressed to stand around in a dusty basement," Trisha said, but Diane said languidly, "Oh, it won't matter."

With a hasty motion Trisha grabbed a towel from the towel drawer. "Suit yourself."

Diane trailed down the steps behind her, and while Trisha closed the circular shower curtain around her and began to undress, Diane grumbled about not finding a chair clean enough to sit on.

"I warned you," Trisha said from behind the curtain and turned on the water, hoping she wouldn't be able to hear Diane's voice.

Unfortunately she could.

Within seconds Diane had launched into a long, involved story about her love life. "At first it was wonderful. Peter demanded so much. He was insatiable, really."

Trisha gritted her teeth and scrubbed at her arms and body vigorously.

"I thought I loved him, but after a while I realized he was boring me. He wanted to spend all his nights in the hot tub—seeing what new things I could think of. I was the one who had to be creative, he wasn't very inventive." A pause. "Nothing like Jord. I was a fool to divorce him."

"I thought you said he insisted on it—because you wanted to keep—your child, and he didn't want children."

Tripped up on the lie, Diane equivocated. "Well, it was a mutual decision."

"That isn't what you told me five years ago."

Diane shot back heatedly, "A few years ago I hadn't been

away from this dismal place long enough to know how the rest of the world lived."

Trisha rinsed the soap off her body and let the water course over her, wetting her hair. "And now you have. What about your job with that electronics firm?"

"Nothing. Dead end. I got tired of it."

Trisha reached for the shampoo. "What a lucky thing that Jord came to your rescue."

Diane's voice brightened. "Yes, isn't it? Switzerland must be lovely this time of year."

Trisha lathered the long length of her hair, feeling bleak, suspended over an abyss. All her fears and insecurities gathered and converged. Her mind pictured them, Jord and Diane in bed, discovering each other, making love. . . . She bent her head and let the water pour over her, sliding her hands over her hair to rinse away the bubbles, and her right hand bumped her other arm. She felt it then, the abrasion on her elbow. She threw back her wet hair, rubbed the water out of her eyes, and twisted her arm to stare at it. The wound was nothing, really, just a series of tiny scratches raised on the sensitive spot near her elbow. But as she stood in the shower staring at those scratches the whole evening came back to her, the bantering, the honesty, the incredible closeness. They had been everything with each other, playful children, confiding friends—and finally lovers. And somehow she knew that anything less wouldn't have satisfied Jord. He would never be content to play the adoring male required by Diane's restless search for self-gratification. He was too intelligent, too sensitive. He hadn't told Trisha he loved her, and she had felt the omission like a pain—but he had wanted to share his life with her. He had told her so. And out of his consideration for her he had left her to make the decision on her own, alone, so that when she came to him, she would have no doubts. . . .

She finished rinsing her hair, wrapped the long bath towel around her body, and stepped out of the shower.

176

Diane gave her a peevish look. "Why don't you do something with that hair. It's so long and—primitive looking. You should get it cut and styled—"

"Some people like it." She smiled, remembering. *Did Lorelei have black hair?*

The tenor of her smile made Diane waspish. "Who likes it? Your tall Texas boyfriend?"

Trisha wrung the water out of her hair. "We've split up." She padded across the floor and began to climb the stairs. Diane followed.

They were in the kitchen when Diane said, "Did you break it off, or did he?"

Trisha kept walking, knowing Diane would follow her up to her bedroom. "I did."

"You're a fool." Diane's voice raked over her nerves like sandpaper. "There aren't any other men around here who are even nominally eligible. You'll be an old maid—"

At the top of the second flight of stairs Trisha turned, nearly knocking Diane down a step. "What an archaic term. As a liberated woman, that's my privilege, isn't it, to decide whether I want to live with a man or spend my life developing my own talents?"

Diane was contemptuous. "What talents?"

Trisha stared back at her, seeing the fine lines that had been carefully covered with makeup, the fight being waged to perserve the illusion of youth. "The talent for living," Trisha answered. She left Diane clinging to the bannister. In her room she dropped the towel and unselfconsciously walked to the dresser to pull out her lingerie. Her sister appeared in the door. Trisha plunged in, hoping she could really swim. "But if what you say is true—then I guess I won't stay here, either." She clipped on her bra, pulled on her underthings, and turned to face Diane. "I'll go to Switzerland with you."

It was particularly pleasant to see Diane's mouth drop open and her forehead draw up in the wrinkles she tried so hard to avoid. "You can't be serious. You—don't have a passport or anything."

"I'll get one."

Shocked again, Diane sank down on the bed. But she did recover—and launched an attack. "Don't be ridiculous," she said in her best derisive tone. "By the time you went through all the red tape, Jord would be back in the States."

Testing, she said, "When is he coming back?"

Diane averted her eyes. "I'm not sure. He didn't say—"

"But he surely mentioned it—so you'd know how much to pack."

Diane gave her an owlish look, so much like Jamie's that Trisha nearly smiled. She guessed that Diane was finding her a more formidable opponent than she had five years ago—and she didn't like it.

"Do you know something I don't?"

Trisha crossed to the closet. "Evidently."

Diane tipped her head downward, the bell of her expertly cut hair brushing her cheek. She raked a fingernail experimentally over the bedspread. "He told you when he was coming back?"

Trisha thrust her legs into khaki pants and brought them up around her slender waist. "Yes." She found a crisp blouse that would be cool and comfortable and slipped it on, tucking it into the waistband.

Diane leaned back and gave her a speculative look under long, artificially lengthened lashes. "Don't tell me Jord finally did something about that—tendresse he's always had for you."

Trisha hid her surprise. "He—had a tendresse for me?"

Diane laughed, a light airy sound that had no substance. "My God, yes. I think you handed him the biggest problem of his young life. He wanted to keep you safe up on your pedestal and take you off in the bushes and ravish you—all at the same time."

It was a rare flash of perception for someone as self-absorbed as Diane, but Trisha guessed it probably came very close to the truth.

"As a matter of fact," Trisha said coolly, "he's asked me to live with him."

There was nothing pretended about the stunned look on Diane's face. Her mouth opened, her eyes widened. Then she threw back her head and laughed. But the laughter was as it had been before, forced, unreal. When she sobered, she gave Trisha a feline smile. "How can that possibly be true when he's asked me to go to Switzerland with him?"

Trisha gave her a straight, steady look. "I'd say at a guess you were lying," she said levelly, "the same way you lied about Jamie being Jord's child."

Trisha watched as Diane visibly fought for control, pushing the emotional pieces inside her head around to rearrange them in some logical order. The Flannery pride surfaced, and the small chin came up. "Well, there certainly has been some major confessing going on while I was gone, hasn't there?"

Trisha said softly, "Don't you want to see him—Jamie?"

Diane's eyes held hers. For a moment Trisha thought she was going to break down. But she didn't.

"I've always made it a point not to window-shop in stores I can't afford," she said with studied casualness and got to her feet. She brushed at imaginary lint on her skirt, her head bent, as if her only concern was her appearance, but when she raised her head, there were tears in her eyes. "You and Margie were the lucky ones. I envied both of you like hell. Somehow I always managed to be in the wrong place at the wrong time."

"You had a wonderful little boy," Trisha said gently. "We all love him."

"I knew you would. I knew he was safe here. I wanted him to be safe. Not like me."

And there, underneath the bright facade, Trisha saw it, the fear and the loneliness that gave rise to Diane's restless seeking. But Diane would not welcome her sympathy. Trisha's voice was gentle. "What will you do now?"

Diane fought with her emotions for a moment. Then, gathering up the scraps of her pride, summoning a bravado that made Trisha's throat fill, Diane blinked eyes that glittered with tears and flashed her most brilliant smile. "I think I'll go downstairs and call Peter. Mother will hardly know I'm home if I don't leave her a long-distance phone bill, will she?"

Diane left the next day. Peter had been ecstatic and agreed to meet her in Chicago. "He'll propose again, I suppose," she had said in a bored tone when she hung up the phone. "This time I might frighten him to death—and accept. It would serve him right."

The heat wave broke, and the rain set in, trapping Trisha in the house. Jamie was told of his adoption, and he seemed to take it well. Since Trisha had discussed placing the farm in Judson's hands, Judson and Margie decided they would move to the larger farmhouse, where they could keep an eye on Virginia as well—so for Jamie the only change would be the absence of his beloved aunt. She knew she would see him often. Jord would see to that. And of course she didn't know just how permanent her liaison with Jord would be. She was his for as long as he wanted her. Beyond that—she refused to think.

With Jamie's future settled and the farm transferred to Judson's capable hands, a restlessness settled over Trisha. She watched the days go by with an impatience that was nearly impossible to contain. As the time neared for Jord to call she was fairly climbing the walls with tension. Suppose Jord changed his mind? Suppose he met someone more beautiful and sophisticated? Suppose he . . . *Stop it,* she told herself sharply. *You've got to trust him. For once—trust him.*

She did trust him. Her confrontation with Diane had shown her that. But—suppose she acted on that trust. Suppose she committed herself irrevocably to Jord in a way that he hadn't asked.

The thought frightened and excited her. But once conceived,

the idea would not let her go. It grew inside her head until it seemed to be the only sensible thing to do. She would not wait here for Jord's phone call. She would perform the act of ultimate trust. She would go to him in New York City.

Once her decision was made, her restlessness left her to be replaced by a nervous anticipation that kept her lying awake all that night. But at least there were things to do. The next day she swung into action. She decided what to pack. She asked Judson to take over the farm work immediately. She called for a reservation on a flight to New York City and asked Judson to take her to the airport.

She had Jord's address. She wouldn't wait for his call. She would be there waiting for him when he came home from Switzerland.

It was raining in New York City when she got out of the cab and climbed the steps to the condominium where Jord lived. She wore a raincoat over the bright-red dress she had bought to bolster her spirits, but as she stood outside the door and rang the buzzer under the awning she could feel where the rain had drizzled through her hair and down under the collar of her coat.

"I'm here to see Mr. Deverone," she told the doorman through the intercom.

"I'm sorry. Mr. Deverone is gone." The voice was flat.

"I know that. But I—that is, please, couldn't I just come in and wait for him?"

There was a hesitation. Then the door swung open, and the doorman, an older man, said crisply, "It's against regulations."

She gnawed her lip in weary frustration. This close to seeing Jord, she couldn't give up. "I'm sure it is," she countered, adopting some of his crispness, "but I'm getting drenched. Look, all I'm asking is that you let me wait in the lobby until he comes in. I—I'm from out of town, and I have nowhere else to go."

"I've heard that line before," he said implacably.

"I'm sure you have," Trisha gritted, "but this time it happens to be true."

Something about her wry unwillingness to be put off must have gotten through to him. "All right," he said gruffly. "I suppose you can wait. But don't go wandering off."

Inside the lobby she dropped her case on the floor and settled into a rather uncomfortable chair. Her week of sleepless nights, her hurried arrangements to make the trip, and her apprehension on the plane had taken their toll, which was why, two hours later, when Jord Deverone came into the lobby, she was sound asleep with her head at an uncomfortable angle.

He didn't see her. Raindrops stood out on his dark coat and glistened in the strands of his gold hair. Distracted, irritated at the delays he had been forced to endure, he strode past the doorman, his head turned as he talked to Brad, his mind going at a fast rate even though he was tired. "I've got to make a telephone call first. Then I'll get the papers you need, and we'll go over them together. . . ."

"Lady waiting for you, Mr. Deverone."

He swore under his breath. If Trisha said yes, and agreed to come to him, this foolish business with other women had to stop. Then he saw her. The breath seemed to leave his lungs. He swore again and said angrily, "Why didn't you let her go up?"

"I couldn't, Mr. Deverone. You said—"

"Never mind what I said." He handed Brad his attaché case and scooped Trisha up into his arms. She awakened, and her eyes flew open in alarm.

Over his shoulder he said, "Grab her suitcase, will you? And get the elevator."

Trisha felt his damp raincoat against her face and smelled the distinct cologne he used, and she wanted to cry with relief at being held in his arms. But he was strangely silent. He stared straight ahead, an angry impatience on his face. He might have been carrying a sack of feed for all the attention he paid her.

Unnerved by his bleak silence, she said tentatively, "Hello," and reached up and traced the lines that seemed to have deepened around his mouth since she had last seen him. "Are you terribly angry with me?"

"No," he muttered and lifted his head as if brushing aside her caress. "Dammit, where is that elevator?"

"It's coming," Brad assured him.

"So is Christmas," Jord snapped.

She was chilled, devastated. He had changed his mind. He didn't want her. "Jord, put me down."

His answer was an even tighter grip on her chest and thighs. She wriggled, trying to push herself free. "Be still," he ordered her brusquely.

With Brad's lively, curious eyes on her there was little else she could do. The elevator arrived at last, and Jord strode into it, carrying her, Brad trailing behind him. When they reached the suite, he said to his assistant, "Unlock the door, will you? The key is in my pocket."

When Brad had done so, Jord told him, "Go on home. I'll talk to you in the morning."

Brad looked at Trisha's cool face as she lay cradled in Jord's arms. Then a strange, almost self-satisfied grin lifted his mouth. "Hello, Miss Flannery. Nice to see you again." And before she could answer, he turned on his heel to stride down the thick carpet back to the elevator doors, whistling as if he were very pleased about something.

Jord swung her inside the apartment. He stood holding her for a moment before he let her slide to her feet. His arm moved upward, and light blazed in his apartment. It wasn't exactly as she had pictured, but nearly so. Plush beige carpeting, a sunken living room, cushy velvet furniture the color of a ripe plum, drapes that would run the length of a barn door draped over what was probably a stunning view of New York. What she hadn't expected to see were the books that filled three walls and the paintings, obviously originals that had been chosen by someone with excellent taste.

"Here, give me that wet coat and go and sit down. I'll get you something to drink."

He helped her take her coat off and gave her a little push toward the stairs.

She didn't move. Instead she turned toward him and watched him hang up her coat and then shrug out of his own. He was slipping out of his suitcoat when she said, "Jord, I—if you want me to leave, just—tell me."

"*Oh, God.*" He threw his jacket on the floor and came to her. Inches away, he gazed at her with something very like pain in his eyes and then groaned and wrapped his arms around her. In that one dazzling moment all her fears disintegrated. "I didn't want it to be like this, you asleep in the chair with exhaustion, me half out of my mind wondering what your answer would be." He kissed her, his mouth warm and gentle and utterly sensual. Then he held her away, and the faintest of smiles touched his mouth. "I was going to clear my work away, come riding up that lane, and carry you away behind Prince."

"I'm sorry I ruined your fantasy," she said and smiled.

"You are my fantasy," he murmured. "You have been since you were—well, thirteen." He gave her a wry smile. "I'm not admitting to any younger than that."

"And you're not angry because I came instead of waiting for your call?" She was confident of his answer.

He feathered a series of slow, erotic kisses along her cheekbone and over her forehead, showing her how ridiculous it was even to ask. "I take it your answer is yes."

"Was I too obvious?"

"Not for me," he groaned. "Never for me." His hands went around to the back of her dress. "What is this?" He was fumbling with the tiny hook at the top of the zipper. "Hooks, zippers? I liked those flimsy little things you wore in Iowa better."

"I could hardly get on a plane to New York wearing a halter top and cutoffs." She let her mouth discover his face, pressing her lips against the fatigue lines along his mouth.

184

"No, I suppose not." He released the hook and slid the zipper down. "You could wear them around the apartment though—for me."

"That sounds ominous—almost like barefoot and pregnant."

His eyes blazed over her. "Now there's an idea. Why didn't I think of that?"

He picked her up once more and carried her down the steps. She was becoming accustomed to being held in his arms, feeling the silk of his shirt next to her cheek. He went up another set of steps and down a hallway to an open door. There was a flare of light, and over his shoulder she caught a glimpse of a bedroom, a very masculine one done in shades of green. The floor reminded her of a plush, grassy lawn. The bed was round, king-size and set on a platform.

He set her down on her feet again, and somehow in the process her dress fell off her shoulders and slid to her feet.

Gently he unclipped her bra and tossed it to the floor, his fingers finding and stripping away her last piece of clothing. "Trisha." His voice sounded choked, deadly serious.

She stepped closer to him and began to unbutton his shirt. "Yes?"

"I—" He made a soft, agonized sound and pressed her down on the bed, half-covering her with his hard body. His chest was heavy on her breasts, a wonderful, remembered weight. "The hell with being reasonable." His mouth took hers, his tongue beginning to create that special ecstasy inside her mouth.

When she could breathe again, she said, "What—reasonable?"

"I was going to wait to tell you that I love you and ask you to marry me. I was going to give you time, give you the chance to see if you could adjust to living in the city. Over the phone I might have managed it—but with you here—" He buried his mouth in the soft center between her breasts. "I want to belong to you. I want to tie us so tightly together you'll never be free."

"Jord." She put a palm against his chest and gently touched his chin with her finger. Love shone from her eyes, glowed from

185

her skin. "You already have. You did that long ago. Of course I'll marry you."

He kissed her fiercely. "Trisha, about Judson—"

"No," she said, pressing her hand against his lips.

He was adamant. "I want to say it this once, and then I won't mention it again. I think I knew you were never involved with him. But when I saw you, first with that Texan and then standing in Jud's arms, kissing him, I went crazy with jealousy. You belonged in my arms, no one else's. I had gone through hell, married Diane to keep you safe and protect you from the gossip and speculation—as well as Virginia. I had finally made up my mind I was going to tell you how much I loved you—when I saw you with Judson—"

She put her fingers on his mouth. "I understand, Jord, really I do. Because I felt the same way. I loved you—that was the reason I lavished so much love and care on Jamie. If I couldn't have you, I could raise your child. But I still couldn't bear the thought of you and Diane—together."

"We never were, you know."

She trailed her finger over his jaw, rough with the day's stubble. "Not according to Diane. I can't believe it wasn't difficult for you."

"I never wanted her. There was only one woman I wanted. But she was a country girl—"

"And you were a city man." She lifted her arm to help him ease out of his shirt. He saw it then, the red marks of the almost-healed scratch on her elbow. "When did you do this?"

"The night we were—swimming."

He chuckled. "I don't remember doing much swimming after you arrived. Shall I kiss it and make it better?"

"It's almost healed—" She stopped. "Yes, would you please?" She laughed up at him, her face glowing with joy, her dark hair spread behind her like a black silky fan on the green satin coverlet, daring him to play out their childish charade. He looked at her, drinking in the reality of her flawless skin, worshiping the

186

beauty of her feminine curves for a long, potent moment. Then he grinned wickedly, accepted her invitation, and pressed his lips against the tiny scar.

Even his mouth on that prosaic part of her body made her shiver with desire. She wanted more, much more. She said seductively, "I have other little aches and pains—"

His eyes glowed. "Where?"

"Well, actually"—she paused as if thinking about it—"I—hurt all over."

He drawled, "Do you really?"

She glanced up at him under dark lashes. "Do you think you can help me?"

"I might," he said. "But it may take years—the rest of your life, in fact."

"I know it will. Oh, darling, I know it will."

LOOK FOR NEXT MONTH'S
CANDLELIGHT ECSTASY ROMANCES ®

THE SEEDS OF SINGING

by Kay McGrath

To the primitive tribes of New Guinea, the seeds of singing are the essence of courage. To Michael Stanford and Catherine Morgan, two young explorers on a lost expedition, they symbolize a passion that defies war, separation, and time itself. In the unmapped highlands beyond the jungle, in a world untouched since the dawn of time, Michael and Catherine discover a passion men and women everywhere only dream about, a love that will outlast everything.

A DELL BOOK   19120-3 $3.95